AUG. 2 0 1985	DATE DUE	
AUG. 2 8 1985		
SEP. 1 0 1985		
NOV. 6 1986		
MAR 6 1987		
OCT 2 7 1987		
JUL 1 6 1990		
DEC 1 8 1990		
MAR 0 6 1992		
APR 2 2 1997		
MAY 2 7 1997		

The Night of
the Scorpion

The Night of the Scorpion

ANTHONY HOROWITZ

PACER BOOKS
a member of The Putnam Publishing Group
New York

Published by Pacer Books,
a member of the Putnam Publishing Group
51 Madison Avenue
New York, NY 10010

Originally published in 1984 by Patrick Hardy Books.
Printed in the United States of America
First American Edition

Library of Congress Cataloging in Publication Data
Horowitz, Anthony, The night of the scorpion.
Summary: An English journalist, his thirteen-year-old
ward, and an Incan boy battle the supernatural evil of
the Old Ones, who plan to enter our world through a
secret gate somewhere in Peru.

PZ7.H7875Ni   1984   [Fic]   84-25518
ISBN 0-448-47751-3

Contents

Prologue

The old man's eyes burned red, reflecting the last flames of the fire. A soft wind ran through his hair, blowing the silver strands around his face. "He will come," he said. "We have no need to send for him. He will come of his own accord."

He got to his feet and stood on the edge of the precipice, turning his back on the four men crouched around the fire. "The boy is on the other side of the world," he continued. "He is thirteen years old."

One of the men stirred uneasily. "How can this boy help us?" he muttered.

"You don't understand, Tomac." The old man turned round. "The boy has power. He is unaware how great his power is, how strong it has become. But it will bring him to us. And although his enemies seek to destroy him, they will only hasten him on his way."

"And what is this boy called?" Tomac demanded.

The old man looked back across the mountains. Far below, the morning mist was rolling along the valleys like a ghostly river.

"His name," he said, 'is Martin Hopkins."

I

Strange Intelligence

Mrs. Hardy took one look round the kitchen, dropped her handbag and sat herself down in a chair. "I don't know," she said, shaking her head mournfully. "Really I don't."

"I'm very sorry, Mrs. Hardy . . ." Richard Cole began.

"Forty years I've been working," the cleaning lady interrupted, "and I've never seen a flat like it. It's not just a mess, Mr. Cole. It's a bloomin' disaster." She fumbled under her dress and pulled out the soggy teabag she had just sat on. On the other side of the table, Martin Hopkins turned his head to hide a smile. "It's a disaster," Mrs. Hardy repeated. "Paper and pens in the linen cupboard. Milk and butter in the desk. And half-frozen socks in the refrigerator. After one morning in this place I have to spend the whole day in bed."

"We do try to keep it tidy," Richard said.

"Well, you don't succeed," Mrs. Hardy sniffed. "Last week I even found a typewriter on the loo. Is that any place to keep a typewriter? It gave me a nasty turn, I can tell you."

It was, without doubt, a curious household. Martin was thirteen. Richard was twenty-six. Martin was at

9

school. Richard worked as a junior reporter on the *Greater Malling Gazette*, a small local newspaper. They had been living in the flat in York, in a street aptly called The Shambles, for almost a month, taking it in turns to cook, clean and wash up. Unfortunately, Richard was hopeless at all three. He couldn't boil an egg without burning a pan or boil a kettle without fusing the lights. As to cleaning and washing up, things had become so bad that Martin had finally persuaded him to pay for a cleaning lady twice a week. Mrs. Hardy had come four times. It seemed unlikely that she would return for a fifth.

"Look, Mrs. Hardy," Richard said with a friendly smile. "If you tidy everything up, we'll really do our best to keep it nice until Friday."

"That's what you said last week."

"Well . . ." Richard glanced at his watch. It was ten past eight in the morning.

"We've got to dash," he said. "We'll talk about it again on Friday." He grabbed his coat while Martin picked up his books. "Can you let yourself out?"

The cleaning lady shook her head. "I just wish I knew how I let myself in for all this."

Once they were in the car, Martin burst into laughter.

"What's so funny?" Richard asked.

"Mrs. Hardy. I know I shouldn't laugh, but the glummer she gets, the funnier she is. And that teabag . . ."

Richard smiled. "She certainly does find it difficult to work us two out," he said. "Last week she asked me what we were doing, living together the way we do."

"What did you tell her?"

"I said I'd adopted you."

Martin considered. "Well," he said, "that's more or less true."

They drove on in silence. As the familiar landmarks flashed by, Martin remembered the events that had brought them together. His own parents had died and he had been taken to a wretched village in Yorkshire. It had been the beginning of a nightmare that might have ended in a freezing quicksand had Richard not arrived and pulled him out. Together they had found themselves fighting an ancient evil—The Old Ones— and it was only at that last moment in the great stone circle of the Devil's Door-bell, that they had finally won.

And now it was all over. Martin was an ordinary schoolboy at a comprehensive just outside York. Richard was still writing for his old newspaper. The two of them never spoke about their adventures.

They drove past a row of shops and a cafe. Martin sorted out his books. In a moment they would pass the garage at the top of a steep hill. Forrest Hill, Martin's school, lay at the bottom on the other side.

"I may be a bit late picking you up," Richard said, changing into low gear.

"That's all right. I can always take the bus. What's up?"

"It's a story. At least, my editor thinks it's a story. 'Vicar hit by falling apple—shock, horror!' You'd think he'd just discovered gravity or something. Why do I have to be the local affairs writer in the one town in England where there are never any local affairs?"

They reached the bottom of the hill and Richard stopped the car. "I'll call by around four-thirty," he said. "Don't wait if a bus comes."

"OK."

"Have a good day. And work hard."

"I always do."

Forrest Hill was a new school, a mass of shining glass and steel forming three sides of a square with a bronze statue of the founder in the middle. It was a mixed school, the youngest pupil eleven, the oldest eighteen. Although Martin had joined after the beginning of term, he had already made plenty of friends. His work wasn't exactly brilliant, but he had been chosen for the junior football team and he had been given a small part in the summer play. All in all, he felt, Forrest Hill wasn't such a bad place—at least as far as schools went.

After he had watched Richard drive away, he turned and began to walk towards the main entrance. He took three steps, then stopped. He brought a hand up to his face and rubbed his brow. It was as if someone had hit him on the side of the head. There was a pounding behind his eyes. His mouth was dry. He took another step and rested against the railings. For a moment he breathed deeply, feeling his heart pounding in his chest.

"What's wrong with you?" he muttered to himself.

Inside the school, a bell rang. Shaking his head, he moved forward. Whatever the matter was, it would clear itself up during the course of the day.

But it didn't. In fact as every minute of the day crawled past, the pain seemed to get worse. It was the last week in May and the sun was shining. To Martin it seemed to be burning. The great glass windows of the classrooms magnified the heat and although many of them were open, the air was close, almost suffocating. By lunchtime, he was wondering if he would be able to get through the rest of the day.

He sat next to his best friend in the dining-hall, a boy of his own age called Robin West.

"What's wrong?" Robin asked, seeing Martin leave his ham salad untouched on the plate.

"It's this heat," Martin complained. "I feel like I'm on fire."

"It isn't hot."

"I'm sweating."

"Well, nobody else is." Robin eyed Martin curiously. "You don't look too good," he said. "In fact you look pretty grim. Maybe you've got some sort of bug."

Martin looked around him. Robin was right. He was the only person in the school who had been affected by the weather. His jacket was on the back of his chair. His shirt was damp. But everyone else was behaving quite normally.

"If I were you," Robin said, helping himself to a tomato from Martin's plate, "I'd go and see the nurse. With a bit of luck, you might get the afternoon off."

"Yes," Martin said, "I think I will."

The nurse was a large woman with uneven teeth and a permanent frown. "Hmmm," she muttered, after she had given him a quick examination, "you are a little feverish. A summer cold, I expect. You'd better not play any games this afternoon."

"Can I go home early?" Martin asked.

"Certainly not!" The matron reached into a drawer and produced two pills. "Take these," she said. "I'm sure you're not going to die if you stay for the last two lessons."

The pills didn't help. Religion and the Sermon on the Mount seemed to go on for ever. He could hardly see the blackboard on the far wall of the classroom and the teacher's voice came over as a meaningless echo, like an announcer in a railway station. It was with great relief that he staggered into the last lesson at three thirty.

It was English literature, which should have been all right except that somehow the teacher managed to make even the most interesting book seem dull and difficult. Mr. Reddy was a tall, elderly man with a thin face and thinning hair. He spoke in a thin, monotonous voice. William Shakespeare was his one love in life. *Macbeth* was the play he was currently dissecting.

> *Double, double toil and trouble;*
> *Fire burn and cauldron bubble.*

The words from Act Four were written on the blackboard and Mr. Reddy was discussing them. "Of course," he was saying, "we no longer believe in witchcraft and black magic today. We would ignore the 'strange intelli-

13

gence' of the weird sisters. But in Shakespeare's time, many people believed in witchcraft. King James himself . . ."

His voice faded into the distance. There was a loud drumming in Martin's ears and the classroom shimmered. Now everything was silent. Slowly, he turned his head towards the window. That was when the horror began.

He saw a lorry, floating through the air, making no sound. There was no driver behind the wheel. Like a great beast it soared towards the school, plummeting out of the sky. Its headlamps were its eyes. The radiator grill was a gaping mouth. The lorry was enormous, a great blue cylinder on twelve thick black tyres. Closer and closer it came. Now it filled up the whole window and was about to smash through . . .

"Hopkins!"

The vision flickered and disappeared as Martin twisted his head round to face an angry Mr. Reddy.

"Yes, Sir?" he said.

"Answer my question, boy."

"I'm sorry, Sir. I didn't hear it."

"I see." Mr. Reddy smiled malignantly. "Other things on our mind, have we? No interest in William Shakespeare? Very well, Hopkins. You will stay behind afterwards and we will find something that will occupy you. Like five hundred lines, for example." He turned to another boy. "Now, West, perhaps you can tell me what the witches meant by . . ."

Martin pressed his fingers against his eyes, trying to clear his head. When he removed them, a second later, the vision had returned. But now it was even more horrible.

The school was on fire. The flames blazed crimson behind the banks of black smoke that filled the classroom. Needle-sharp fragments of glass swirled round in a deadly storm. All the desks were up-turned, with paper everywhere. He could see Robin West, lying with his eyes closed, a pool of blood forming around his head. Mr. Reddy was standing with his back to the wall, clutching his arm. There were people running everywhere, some of them beating at their burning clothes. One girl had plunged into a jagged hole that had opened in the floor. Another was trapped underneath a bookcase that had fallen onto her legs. But still everything was silent. He could see the screams without hearing them. It was like watching a television picture with the sound turned off.

Martin pushed his desk away from him and got to his feet, covering his eyes.

"Yes, Hopkins?" Mr. Reddy asked, pausing in mid-sentence.

Martin looked up. The classroom was normal again. But he knew now that it wouldn't be for long.

"What do you want, boy," the teacher demanded impatiently.

"I'm sorry, Sir," Martin said, trying to keep his voice steady. Somebody sniggered. "You've got to get everyone out of here."

"Out of here? Are you proposing a nature trail, Hopkins? What exactly do you mean?"

"I can't explain, Sir. But something terrible is going to happen. Soon. You've got to evacuate the school."

Mr. Reddy stared at Martin, his face caught between anger and astonishment. The rest of the class were talking amongst themselves now, laughing at Martin's expense.

"Be quiet!" the teacher shouted.

Then, more quietly, he asked, "Is this your idea of a joke, Hopkins?"

"No, Sir."

"Because if you think you're being funny, I can assure you . . ."

"I don't, Sir. Please, Sir . . ."

"Sit down, Hopkins. We will discuss this later." Mr. Reddy paused, his face going the colour of his name. "Sit down I say!"

It was useless. Martin stepped out from behind his desk and, before anyone could stop him, ran to the back of the classroom and punched at a panel of glass set in the wall. It was the fire-alarm. Instantly, bells sounded throughout the school. Along the corridors, doors opened. Feet stamped down the stairs. Martin's own class hesitated for a moment, but the rules for fire drill were the same, whatever the circumstances. As one, they slammed their books shut and made for the door. Martin followed them, Mr. Reddy close behind.

The teacher caught up with him in the football field. By now, the school was empty. All the classes were assembling outside in pre-arranged groups and a head count was being made. Martin didn't protest as Mr. Reddy took him by the back of the neck and dragged him over to where a bewildered headmaster stood, waiting for either the flames or the fire brigade to appear.

"Mr. Reddy," he said, seeing the teacher, "do you know what's going on?"

"Yes, Headmaster," Mr. Reddy replied. "I'm sorry, but it's a false alarm. This boy here—Hopkins—he set off the bell as some sort of prank."

"A prank?" The headmaster glowered.

"Yes, Headmaster. I'd just punished him for . . ."

But then Mr. Reddy stopped. The headmaster was no longer listening to him. Nor was he looking at him. He was looking past him. Slowly, the English teacher turned round.

The petrol tanker had been parked at the top of the hill, outside the garage. The driver had crossed the road to the cafe to get something to eat before emptying his tanks. He had been sitting at a table when it happened. A light breeze had played around the lorry. Inside the empty cabin, the brake handle had clicked, then gently lowered itself forward as if moved by an invisible hand. The lorry had rolled forward, picking up speed on the steep hill.

The tanker, out of control and carrying thousands of gallons of petrol was hurtling towards the school. Nothing on earth could stop it.

The impact when it came was deafening. The lorry crashed through the school, snapping the metal supports and sending glass whirling through the air in a thousand pieces. Effortlessly it ploughed through, disappearing into a glittering chaos. For a moment, after it had buried itself in the building, all was still. Then it exploded. A fireball erupted out of the wreckage, shooting into the sky, threatening to singe the very clouds. The intense heat even reached the football field, two hundred yards away. Flames rushed out of what was left of the school, searing the grass and concrete all round.

"My God!" the headmaster croaked. "If we had been in there . . ."

"He knew!" Mr. Reddy let go of Martin and backed away. "He knew before it happened," he whispered. "Hopkins knew."

The headmaster looked at him, his eyes wide. If Martin had expected gratitude, he was disappointed. The man's face was filled with fear.

The rest of the school began to find out what had taken place before the collision. The pupils in Martin's class were spreading the story. Eyes were turned on him. Excited whispers were exchanged. There was nervous laughter. But nobody spoke to him. When he walked over towards his friends, they slunk away as though he were diseased.

Richard arrived twenty minutes later. There were still flames flickering in the wreckage of the school. Martin was completely surrounded by staff, police and firemen as well as journalists and photographers who had descended on the school from every direction.

"Martin!" Richard ran over and pulled him away from the crowd. "Are you all right?"

Martin gave a small smile. "I'm fine now. I'm glad you're here. Have you heard what happened?"

Richard nodded. "I heard it on the radio. I'm sorry. I'd have got here sooner but I was miles away." He glanced at the ruins of the school. "If it hadn't been for you, people would have died. What a horrible accident . . ."

"Accident?" Martin kicked at a charred exercise book lying on the concrete. "Do you really think it was an accident?"

"Of course. What else could it have been?"

Martin turned back and took a last look at what remained of Forrest Hill. He shivered. "Let's go home," he said.

2

The Mad Monk

"Of course it was an accident."

"I don't know, Richard. I wish it was, but . . . but as soon as you'd gone, I *knew* something was going to happen. It's difficult to explain. But I'm certain that the lorry wasn't aimed at the school. It was aimed at me."

"But how can you say that, Martin?"

"I don't know." Martin sighed. "How do you explain something that's happening inside you? But I promise, I was the one it was aimed at."

"Why?"

"Because somewhere, something is going to happen. And I'm not meant to be there when it does."

The kitchen clock ticked round to six o'clock. Outside, it was growing dark. It had been drizzling all day, a depressing end to the month of May. In one corner of the room, a black-and-white television set stood on a chair. It was turned on, but neither Richard nor Martin was watching it. An announcer was reading the news.

The Prime Minister flew home early today after an extended visit to Washington where, it is believed . . .

Four days had passed since the Forrest Hill incident.

The Night of the Scorpion

Richard and Martin were sitting at the kitchen table, drinking tea. The journalist's flat was even more of a mess than usual. Mrs. Hardy should have called in that morning. But when the Forrest Hill story had been blazed across the front pages of all the local and national newspapers, she had telephoned to say she would no longer be coming.

They had been four terrible days for Martin. First, there had been the enquiry. The lorry driver had sworn that he had left the lorry with the brakes firmly on. An expert who had examined the wreckage had then testified that there was nothing wrong with the brakes' mechanism but that they had been left off. Then Mr. Reddy had appeared. It was his version of the story that had started the furore, a version that a dozen witnesses had verified.

Three times Martin had been taken to York police station to be questioned and requestioned about his role in the Forrest Hill affair. At times he had been made to feel that he had in some way caused the collision. More experts had been called up from London to conduct tests on him, using cards with queer signs and a whole mass of electronic equipment. Martin had tried to help, but the tests had been unsuccessful and eventually the police had told him that he needn't come back.

But the affair wasn't over yet. There were still dozens of newspapermen surrounding the flat, hoping for a glimpse of Martin. The telephone hadn't stopped ringing and Richard had been forced to leave it off the hook. Too many questions had been asked. Too few answers had been given.

Yorkshire police have released no further information about the Forrest Hill school incident earlier this week in which . . .

Richard had taken the week off to look after a friend. It hadn't been an easy time for him either. Once his editor had found out that he was living with the hottest story in the country, he had demanded a front-page exclusive. But much as Richard would have enjoyed writing it, he knew how Martin felt. He had refused. And now it was uncertain whether he would have a job to return to.

Richard dipped a biscuit into his tea and sucked thoughtfully. "What we need right now," he said, "is a holiday."

"Where?"

"Anywhere, as long as it's far away. If we just disappear for a couple of weeks, everyone will forget about Forrest Hill. How do you like the sound of . . . Paris? Or maybe Rome?"

Martin sat in silence, half-watching the flickering pictures on the television. Richard lit a cigarette.

And finally, in Sotheby's tomorrow, there is to be an unusual sale of rare books. The most peculiar item in the collection is the diary of the so-called Mad Monk of Cordova . . .

Martin started forward. His hand, still holding his cup, splashed tea onto the table.

'What's the matter?' Richard asked.

"Didn't you see it?" Martin demanded.

"See what?"

"The news. I wasn't listening. But I saw it, Richard. I saw it."

"What did you see, Martin?" Richard looked at the television. The news had ended and a sad-looking weatherman was pinning magnetic clouds all over a map of England.

Martin stood up, his eyes full of excitement. "You'll see," he said.

There wasn't another broadcast until nine o'clock that night, but when the hour arrived, Richard and Martin were sitting in front of the television set, watching it intently. Once again the newscaster went through the day's stories: the Prime Minister in Washington, an airport strike in Paris, Forrest Hill.

"This is the story," Martin said.

A picture of Sotheby's, the London auction house, had flashed up on the screen.

In Sotheby's tomorrow, the newscaster's voice commentated, *there is to be an unusual sale of rare books. The most peculiar item in the collection is the diary of the so-called Mad Monk of Cordova. The book, formerly believed to be lost, was written by one of the original Spanish conquistadors who invaded Peru and defeated the Incas in 1532. The author's true name is unknown. He went mad in Peru, returned to Spain and wrote the book in a monastery in Cordova shortly before he died. The diary, bound in leather and gold, is a fantastic medley of fact and fantasy . . .*

"It's coming now," Martin said. The diary had appeared on the screen. It was about the size of a hymn book, bound in a thick leather cover with a golden scorpion engraved on the front.

. . . and appears to contain many remarkable predictions about the future, including the coming of motor cars, satellites and computers. It even goes so far as to predict the complete destruction of Peru!

"There!" Martin cried.

Richard stared. Under the rather mocking voice of the newscaster, the film had shown the inside of the monk's diary, the pages being flicked over by someone's hand. It had only been a fleeting glimpse but as the pages had turned, the camera had paused on one of them. Half the page had been covered in large letters, and underneath them there had been a design. Richard had only been able to see it for a second, but there could be no mistaking it:

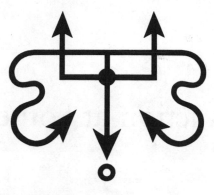

"You saw it?" Martin said.

"Yes," Richard replied. "I saw it."

"And you know what it is?"

"Of course I know what it is." The journalist stood up and flicked the television off. "It's the sign of The Old Ones."

3
An Auction at Sotheby's

Richard and Martin climbed up the stairs from New Bond Street and plunged into the curious world that was Sotheby's, one of London's most famous auction houses. Looking around him, Martin couldn't help feeling that he had wandered into some incredible lost property office. Shelves full of Victorian dolls gave way to row upon row of Chinese maps and charts. Pictures of all shapes and sizes lined the walls. And every single object carried a brown, numbered label as if it were waiting to be claimed by whichever careless eccentric had misplaced it.

The main auction room of Sotheby's, a large hall with faded green wallpaper and a drab grey carpet, was already more than half full, although the rare book sale wasn't due to begin for another twenty minutes. At the far end, an antique wooden podium with a microphone attached awaited the auctioneer. An electronic display overhead listed the value of the pound in six currencies and earnest-looking men and women sat in rows, checking the figures on pocket calculators. As dozens of clocks (themselves labelled and due to be sold the next day) ticked on and the time of the sale moved closer, more and more people entered the room and took their places to wait for the start of the bidding.

Behind the auctioneer's stand, a long table had been set up, groaning under the weight of a great pile of books. Richard and Martin made for it, muttering their apologies as they pushed through the rows of chairs. An assistant was standing at one end of the table and had seen them coming. He gave them the polite but un-enthusiastic smile that he reserved for people who were obviously not serious bidders.

"Excuse me," Richard began.

"Yes, Sir?"

"We wondered if it would be possible to look at a book."

The assistant simpered at them. "There are well over two hundred books here for you to look at, Sir."

"I meant one particular book," Richard said.

"The diary," Martin added. "The diary of the mad monk."

The assistant rubbed his hands together as though he were washing them. "I'm afraid that's not possible," he said. "The diary is one of the most valuable books in the collection and is not on public display. Now if you'll excuse me . . ." With a little nod, he walked off in the direction of a portly Arab who was trying to find a seat.

"So much for that!" Martin muttered.

"Don't give up too quickly," Richard said.

"What can we do?"

"Not a lot right now. But somebody's got to buy the diary. Let's stay and watch the bidding."

They turned round and found themselves facing a small, sallow-skinned man who had evidently overheard their brief conversation. He was only a little taller than Martin with brown hair that was thinning as fast as it was fading in colour. He had narrow, nervous eyes and thin lips. He was dressed in pale yellow trousers, a pink cardigan and a grey, spotted bow-tie.

"Excuse me," he said. "May I . . . I didn't mean to eavesdrop . . . but what is your interest in the diary?"

"We want to look at it," Richard told him.

"Yes. I heard. But . . . forgive me . . . you don't look like an antique dealer."

"I'm not. Are you?"

The little man nodded. "Yes. My name is David Goodge . . . of Goodge Antiques."

"Well, let's just say that we have an interest in the diary," Richard said. "We want to see who buys it."

"Oh . . . I intend to buy it," Goodge said. He rubbed his chin. "I *will* buy it."

"Will you let us have a look at it?" Martin asked.

"I'm afraid not. No. I'm sorry . . ."

"Well what do you intend to do with it?" Richard asked.

"I intend to destroy it."

Richard and Martin watched the sale begin from the back of the hall. It was a brisk business. Two men were responsible for displaying each object while a third, the auctioneer, gave a brief description and then opened the bidding. One after another the books were sold, some for only a hundred pounds, others for several thousand. Martin watched the bidding curiously. Without the experienced eye of the auctioneer, he found it hard to say who was bidding for what. A hand was moved here, an eyebrow there, a head nodded or a pencil was raised. With each tiny gesture, the bidding leapt up. And as the hammer fell and the books were sold, the crowd bent low over their catalogues, pens scribbling as they took notes. In a way the sale was exciting. It was just that nobody who was involved in it seemed particularly excited.

Then the auctioneer announced Lot 1108 and the diary was brought in. The excitement became visible in the faces of the bidders. Glances were exchanged, pocket calculators consulted. Only the auctioneer himself kept a completely blank expression as though he had no interest whatsoever in the proceedings. "Lot 1108," he announced, his voice amplified by the microphone. "The diary of the Mad Monk of Cordova, handwritten and dated 1554. The diary is one hundred and seventy-three pages long in a leather cover decorated with an inlaid gold scorpion motif. I am opening the bidding at twenty thousand pounds."

Martin watched carefully as the bidding rose. Thirty thousand, forty thousand . . . it was impossible to see where each bid came from. He gave up and concentrated instead on David Goodge. The antique dealer was sitting next to the centre aisle, one leg crossed over the other, one hand resting on his knee. He seemed to be as still as a statue, but then Martin saw his little finger twitch. It was a tiny movement, but it had not escaped the auctioneer's eye. "Ninety thousand pounds," he called out.

Suddenly Martin wanted the dealer to buy the book, and once he had recognized the fact, he found himself totally caught up in the sale. The hair on the back of his neck prickled as the figures rose. Already the diary was commanding a hundred and fifty thousand pounds. Who could possible afford such an astronomical sum? Was it the Arab, sitting in the front row? Or the woman in black sitting just behind Goodge? The auctioneer's head swung round to the left. "Two hundred thousand pounds," he said. Who had made the bid? Nobody was giving anything away.

The bids reached two hundred and fifty thousand pounds. There was a long silence.

"Going . . . !" the auctioneer announced.

Martin looked anxiously around the crowd. He hadn't been able to see if Goodge had made the bid himself. Had the price been too much for the antique dealer?

"Going . . . !"

He wanted to bid for the diary himself. It was a crazy idea, of course, but he could feel his arm twitching. To be so near the diary and yet so far was nothing less than torture.

"Gone!" The hammer banged down. "Sold to Mr. David Goodge for two hundred and fifty thousand pounds."

There was a scattering of applause. The antique dealer slumped back in his chair, a smile flickering on his lips.

"Two hundred and fifty thousand pounds," Richard whispered. "That's one hell of a lot to pay for a book you mean to destroy."

Richard and Martin waited outside until the sale had finished and the crowd had broken up. A few minutes later, the antique dealer appeared, holding a briefcase close to his chest.

"Mr. Goodge?" Richard called out, running over to him.

The antique dealer started back, then relaxed when he saw who it was. "I am in a bit of a rush . . ." he muttered.

"Please, Sir," Richard said. "The book . . ."

"No." Goodge clutched the case even more tightly. "It has nothing to do with you."

"It has everything to do with us," Martin cried. "The Old Ones . . ."

The words had an awful effect on the little man. He fell back, his eyes staring. It was as if he had just been given the news of his own death. "What do you know about them?" he asked.

"They're creatures," Martin said. "Devils. They were in the world at the beginning of time. Then they were expelled and a gate was built to keep them out. The gate was called the Devil's Door-bell and it was in Yorkshire. They wanted to break the gate, to come into the world, to destroy it."

"How do you know all this?" the antique dealer demanded.

"Because I had to fight them," Martin said. "I won, but now, somehow, they've come back. They tried to kill me. At Forrest Hill . . ."

David Goodge stared at him in wonderment. "I thought I knew your face," he said. "In the papers . . . you were the boy . . ."

"That's right," Martin said.

The antique dealer wiped his brow with a trembling hand. "Then you are one of those who know," he said. "The Devil's Door-bell. Yes. Everything you say is true. But there's something you don't know. You say that one gate was built, in Yorkshire. But there is another . . . in South America . . . in Peru."

"A second gate," Richard muttered.

"That's right." Now the antique dealer spoke quickly, his voice low. "One of the men who sailed with Pizarro and the conquistadors to Peru discovered it in his travels around the country. It was that discovery that drove him mad. Not only did he find the gate, he found a way that it could be opened. It came to him in a vision . . . and that's what he wrote down here." He tapped the briefcase. "Now do you see why I had to buy it? The secret has to be destroyed . . . even if it means burning the whole diary."

"I still have to see it," Martin said.

"Can't we just have a quick look?" Richard asked.

Goodge looked left and right. The auction house was almost empty now, but there were still a few people making their way out. "Not here," he said. He fumbled in his pocket and produced a bent visiting card. "Come to my shop this evening. At eight o'clock."

"Why not before?" Martin asked.

"So that I can find out if you are who I think you are."

"And who do you think I am?"

"The prophecy . . ." Goodge said, "surely you know . . . the five . . ."

"Mr. Goodge?"

The three of them wheeled round.

There was something very horrible about the man who stood before them, something almost inhuman. He was tall and well-built with blond, curling hair. He was dressed in a smart blue blazer and white trousers which were slightly crumpled as though he had been sitting in them for a long time. But it was his face that was somehow wrong. The skin seemed to have been stretched too tight, distorting his eyes and freezing his mouth. In places it was a blotchy red where the sun had attempted to give it some kind of tan. His eyes were a watery green, a colour made more ugly by the fact that the man had no eyebrows.

"Mr. Goodge?" the man enquired again.

"Yes?" The antique dealer edged closer to Richard as if for protection.

"Forgive me for interrupting your conversation." The man spoke in a strong German accent. His voice was as cold as his appearance. "My name is Todd."

"Todd?"

"Mr. Todd. I am informed that you have just purchased a diary."

"Perhaps."

"Could you perhaps spare me a few minutes to talk privately with you?"

"What about?"

The German looked at Richard and Martin. Almost at once, his eyes dismissed them. He turned again to David Goodge. "I have come a long way to get here," he said. "Many thousands of miles, in fact. It was my intention to purchase the diary. I would have been here early this morning but for an airport strike in Paris which delayed my connection. Nonetheless, I am still interested in buying the diary."

"I'm sorry," Goodge said. "It's not for sale."

The man's lips twisted upwards in a parody of a smile. "You don't understand," he said. "I am willing to make you a quite remarkable offer. Twice what you paid for it."

"I'm sorry, Mr. Todd," the antique dealer repeated. "And I'm sorry, you've come all this way for nothing. I am keeping the diary."

Mr. Todd stepped forward. Martin shivered. There was something deadly in his eyes.

"I would advise you to think again," he said.

"Are you threatening me?" Goodge asked.

"I make no threats. However . . ."

"Look," Richard interrupted. "It's obvious that Mr. Goodge doesn't want to sell. Why don't you just leave quietly?"

The man's head whipped round; then he stepped back and bowed. "Very well," he said. "I shall say no more now." He turned once again to the antique dealer. "But if I were you," he said, "I would remember my name." And with that he was gone.

A few minutes later, the antique dealer left too, leaping into the first taxi that came along. As the driver began to pull away, he opened the window and leant out.

"Come tonight!" he said. "And come by yourselves. You see . . . I was right. The diary has to be destroyed."

Richard and Martin were left alone on the pavement. Together they set off in search of a coffee.

"Todd was a nasty piece of work," Martin said as they walked.

"Yes." Richard was deep in thought. "Mr. Todd . . . Mr. Todd . . ."

"Do you know the name?" Martin asked.

"No. It's just . . . well, he spoke with a German accent."

"So what?"

"Well, I learnt German once. I still remember a few words. *Der Tod*, for example."

"What does it mean?"

"There may be nothing to it. But it just happens to be the German word for death."

4

A Murder in Chelsea

It was dark by the time Richard and Martin reached Chelsea. Goodge Antiques was situated in a quiet cul-de-sac behind the King's Road, not far from the river. It was an antique shop in more senses than one. The building itself looked about three hundred years old with ivy growing up the walls, a curving oak door with an iron handle and a latticed display window that slanted at an odd angle from the ground. The window was crammed with curious objects, all of them from various parts of South America. Ugly wooden statues glared out from behind multi-coloured maps and scrolls. A row of hand-painted vases stood beside a twisting pottery trumpet, fashioned to look like a snake. There were necklaces, brooches, knives and chisels, all thrown together haphazardly. A sign reading *Closed* hung against the glass. There were no lights on inside the shop.

Richard pulled at the iron chain beside the door and stepped back as a bell chimed somewhere inside. There was no answer. He waited a minute and rang again. Still there was no response.

"I don't like this," Martin said.

"Relax. He's probably working in a room at the back."

Richard rang for a third time, then pushed at the door. It was locked. "Come on," he said.

A narrow alley ran between Goodge Antiques and the neighbouring shop. They followed it, Richard peering through the windows as they went. About half-way along the building they came to a second door. Richard knocked, then knelt down and looked through the letter-box.

"There's no-one around," he said, "but it's a Yale lock. Your arm is thinner than mine. Maybe you can open it."

"Do you think we ought to?" Martin asked.

"No, I don't." Richard shrugged. "But in for a penny . . ."

Martin rolled up his sleeve and forced his arm through the letter-box, the metal rim biting into his flesh. Bending it round, he stretched for the lock.

"Can you reach it?" Richard asked.

"No. It's too far."

"Push with your shoulder."

Taking a deep breath, Martin pushed forward. His arm felt as though it was being twisted off, but somehow his fingers reached the knob. He felt it turn. Then the door swung open and he gingerly disentangled himself from the letter-box. They were in.

The side door led into a small kitchen. Richard found a light switch and turned it on. A single bulb, hanging without a shade, lit up the room which was bare but for a fridge and a gas-ring. Only one door led out. Treading softly, the two of them moved forward and opened it.

"Mr. Goodge?" Richard called. Apart from the ticking of a clock, all was silent.

From the kitchen they passed into the main body of the shop which was far larger than they had thought.

Like the window, it was madly cluttered up with all sorts of bits and pieces from South America: idols and totem poles, pots and vases, woven cloths and metal spears. An ornate grandfather clock stood against a wall, completely surrounded by old leather books on sloping shelves. The whole place was such a jumble of bric-a-brac that Martin wondered how the antique dealer ever managed to find anything.

"Come on," Richard whispered.

They walked farther in. Beside the front door, a giant wooden gargoyle seemed to follow their movements with huge, bulging eyes. The ticking of the clock echoed in the gloom like a metallic heart-beat. A strange, musty smell filled the air.

"What are we looking for?" Martin whispered.

"I wish I knew," Richard said.

Another door opposite the kitchen and half-hidden by a thick, velvet curtain, led into what might have been the shop's office. It was slightly ajar and they could see a chink of light creeping through the gap. More quietly now, afraid of what they might find, they pulled the curtain back and went into the room.

It was indeed an office. It was furnished with a large, mahogany desk, a wardrobe and two filing cabinets. A picture depicting a Mexican temple had been removed from the wall to reveal a small safe. The safe was open. An anglepoise lamp stood on a table, throwing long shadows across the floor.

David Goodge was slumped across the desk, one hand stretched out as if reaching for something. He was dead; his body still and his fingers rigid. Richard swore under his breath and went over to the man. A moment later he looked up. "He's been strangled," he said.

Martin swallowed. "What about the diary?" he asked.

Richard glanced at the wall. "The safe's empty."

Richard was standing by the desk, Martin by the

door. The wardrobe creaked. Both of them looked at it. Suddenly the door flew open and a figure leapt out, spun a knife round in his hand, seized hold of the blade and hurled it at Richard. At the same time, he started for the door. But he hadn't seen Martin. Martin, acting instinctively, grabbed hold of his arm. The man brought his other hand up, still clutching the leather-bound diary. The side of his fist hit Martin on the jaw and he was sent flying. As he fell, there was a ripping sound and part of the man's jacket was torn open. Then Martin was on the floor, calling out to Richard, while the man ran out through the antique shop.

Groggily, Martin got to his feet and looked up at Richard. He gazed in horror. The journalist was standing against the wall, the hilt of the knife jutting out of his neck.

"Richard . . ." he cried.

But then, with a deep sigh, the journalist stepped aside. The knife remained, stuck in the wall. It had missed him by a fraction of an inch.

"Are . . . you OK?" he asked.

Martin fingered the side of his mouth. "I'll live."

"Did you see who it was?"

"No. He was too fast. But . . ."

"The man from the auction house," Richard said. He looked at the knife. "Let's get out of here."

"Wait a minute."

Martin reached down and picked up something that he had seen fall from the German's pocket during their brief struggle. It was a biro; a cheap, plastic thing, the sort that banks and other businesses give away. Engraved beside the clip were two red letters and a word in black:

TC (Lima)

"Lima . . ." Martin read, handing the biro to Richard.

"The capital of Peru." Richard slipped the biro into

36

his pocket and took one last look at the dead antique dealer. "Let's go home," he said.

Martin sat thoughtfully as the train rattled through the night on the way back to York. His mouth was bruised, the skin tender, but there was no serious damage. Richard sipped beer out of a can and nibbled a stale British Rail cheese sandwich. The biro lay on the table beside them, rocking back and forth with the movement of the train.

At last Martin spoke. "I want to go to Peru," he said.

Richard paused, the can half way to his lips. "I had a nasty feeling you were going to say that."

"I have to go," Martin insisted. It was a simple statement of fact.

"And how are we going to pay for the tickets?" Richard asked.

"You've got money saved."

"Thanks very much. I also have a job and a mortgage." Richard put the can down. "Be honest, Martin," he said. "Is this really any of our business? Do we have to get involved?"

With a roar, the train plunged into a tunnel. When it emerged, Martin was leaning forward, holding the biro. "You heard what Mr. Goodge said," he began. "There's another gate, in Peru, and it's going to open. He knew it. And Mr. Todd knows it too. That's why he took the diary." He lifted the biro. "I bet it's already half way to Lima by now."

"But that doesn't mean . . ."

"Richard, I've got to go. I wish I didn't have to. I just want to go to school like everybody else and have fun and all the rest of it. But I can't just ignore what's happening . . . my power. Forrest Hill only happened because of me. The Old Ones were afraid that I'd stop them so that's why they did what they did. They didn't

37

care how many people died as long as they killed me.
I'm certain of it. I've beaten them once and they're afraid
that I'll do it again. So I have to go. You don't have to
come with me if you don't want to. But . . . well . . . do
you think you could lend me the fare?"

Richard crumpled the beer can in his hand. Sticky
brown liquid frothed out of the top and onto the table.
"All right, all right," he said, shaking his fingers. "Suppose
we do go to Peru. What are we supposed to do
when we get there?"

"Look for the gate."

"But what exactly do we look for?"

"A circle of stones. A temple or something. I don't
know . . ."

"And here's another thing. We know that the gate is
going to open soon. But we don't know when. Suppose
it happens tomorrow? Suppose we arrive too late?"

"That's just a chance we've got to take."

There was a long silence. The train raced through a
station, blurred lights sweeping past the windows. "All
right," Richard said at last. "If you want to go to Peru,
off you go. But let me tell you this, my friend. If you
think you're going alone, you're out of your tiny mind.
Although you frequently seem to forget the fact, you're
only thirteen years old. And let's just remember that
Peru does happen to be round the other side of the world.
Somebody has to look after you and like it or not—and
I assure you I don't like it one little bit—it looks like I'm
the only person around who's silly enough to volunteer.
So if you go, I go. Right?"

"Right." Martin smiled.

Richard shrugged. "Oh well," he said, "it was only
yesterday that I was saying we needed a holiday."

5
Flight VA 920

"This is your captain speaking. We are cruising at an altitude of 35,000 feet and at a speed of four hundred miles an hour. The plane will be making brief stop-overs in Paris, Madrid, Caracas and Bogota before flying on to Lima. There is a little stormy weather forecast over South America, but nothing to worry about. I hope you enjoy the flight."

Richard Cole wasn't enjoying the flight one little bit. He was sitting near the Emergency Exit door, his left hand curled around his knee, his right hand clutching not one but three St. Christopher medallions. His face was a curious shade of green.

"I didn't know you were scared of flying," Martin said.

"I'm not scared of flying," Richard replied. "I'm scared of planes."

"What's the difference?"

"I break into a cold sweat when I even look at a plane," Richard explained. "It doesn't have to fly. I even got air-sick in the duty free shop."

The DC10 had taken off from Heathrow Airport at half-past seven in the evening. Now there were twenty hours' travelling ahead of them with a change of planes at Caracas airport in Venezuela.

With a soft chime, the *No Smoking* light blinked out above their heads. Richard sighed with relief and reached for his duty free cigarettes. When, a few minutes later, a stewardess appeared pushing a trolley of drinks, he perked up considerably. And by the time he had got two whiskies inside him, with a third lined up in front of him, he was quite his old self.

"It's years since I learnt Spanish," he said, opening a phrase book which he had bought in a second-hand bookshop in Yorkshire. "But that's the only language they understand in Peru. Fortunately, I have a wonderful accent. Listen to this. *Una cabra say commy-o mee passaporty.* There you are! What do you think of that?"

"It sounded wonderful," Martin said. "What does it mean?"

"Er—a goat has eaten my passport." Richard shrugged. "You never know. It may come in useful."

He shut the book and brought out a guide to Peru that he had found in the same shop.

"What will we do when we get to Lima?" Martin asked.

"I'm not exactly sure," Richard admitted. "I suppose the first thing is to book into a hotel and start getting to know the place. Then we can look for TC—whatever that means."

"It must be some sort of business."

Richard took the biro out of his pocket and rolled it between his fingers. "Whatever it is, it's a pretty thin lead," he said. "Let's just hope it leads somewhere . . . and soon."

"If only we'd seen more of the book," Martin said.

"If only we'd never seen anything of the book!" the journalist sighed, settling back into his seat.

The man with the silver hair closed the book and looked up. "You have done very well, Mr. Todd." He spoke in Spanish, his voice thin and high-pitched. "It is unfortunate that you were not able to buy the diary in the conventional manner, but what matters is that we have it." He slid the diary into the top drawer of his desk and locked it. "There was no trouble with the English police?"

"I was out of the country before the antique dealer was found," Mr. Todd assured him.

"Good."

The two men were sitting in a large, expensively furnished office on the ninth floor of a building in Lima. It was half-past three in the afternoon. The man facing Mr. Todd was dressed in an immaculate suit with black, brightly polished shoes and tinted, silver-framed glasses. His skin was dark, his eyes grey. He was an unusually short man—only a little over five feet tall—and everything in the office had been scaled down to suit him. The seats were all a little too low to be comfortable for an ordinary person. The legs of the desks and tables had had a few inches sawn off to shorten them. Even the door had been built so that Mr. Todd had been forced to bend down as he walked in.

The German sipped at a drink, feeling the cold glass between his fingers. "There is one thing . . ." he began.

"Yes?"

"I did have a little trouble in . . ."

The other man slammed his fist down on the table. "I do not like the word 'little'!" he snarled. "You will not use that word when you are speaking to me!"

"I'm sorry." Mr. Todd's lips twitched. "I did have a . . . certain amount of trouble in London. Nothing serious, but . . ."

"Tell me."

"There were two people at the antique dealer's. They surprised me there just after I had seen to him. I think they were after the diary. I had seen them earlier that day at the auction. A man and a boy."

The silver-haired man cupped his hands together. "Curious."

"It's more curious than you think," Mr. Todd continued. "The boy is called Martin Hopkins. The man is a journalist; Richard Cole. As it happens, Hopkins was on the front page of every newspaper three days before I arrived in England."

Mr. Todd reached into his pocket and pulled out a newspaper clipping which he handed to the other man. The Peruvian opened it and read.

DID SCHOOLBOY SEE INTO THE FUTURE?

It could be one of the most important instances of clairvoyance, precognition or "second sight" ever placed on record. Unlike many other similar cases, there were dozens of witnesses. Nobody is denying that a major catastrophe with considerable loss of life was narrowly averted.

But as ever when the paranormal is under discussion, the issue is still surrounded by controversy. Did thirteen-year-old Martin Hopkins really display some sort of strange power that enabled him to save the staff and eight hundred pupils at the Forrest Hill School in Yorkshire? Or is there another explanation?

The facts—in so far as they are known—are as follows ...

Above the article describing the events at Forrest Hill, there was a photograph of Martin taken outside the school. As the Peruvian gazed at it, the colour drained from his face. His fingers tightened on the paper. "This boy," he muttered, "and the journalist ..."

"They left London for Lima a few hours ago," Mr. Todd interrupted. "I had two of my men watch all the flights from Heathrow." He shrugged. "Just in case."

The Peruvian shook his head. "You did well, Mr. Todd," he said. "But then foresight always was one of your strong points."

"Do you want me to kill them?"

The Peruvian shook his head. "No. I don't know how much they know. Killing them might only draw attention to ourselves." He pursed his lips. "They will change planes at Caracas?"

"Yes."

"Can you have someone on the plane for the last stretch to Lima?"

"No problem."

"Good."

The Peruvian stood up and walked over to the window that had been built closer to the ground than usual. Far below him, the afternoon traffic moved thick and slow through the streets of Lima. "It is absolutely critical that the boy does not set foot in Lima," he said. "If he is who I suspect he is, he could ruin everything. But I have an idea. By the time we have finished with him, he will be powerless to stop us."

Giggling, he snatched a bottle up off the table. "Another drink, Mr. Todd?"

The German raised his glass. "Just a lit . . ." He swallowed hard and blinked. "Not for me, thank you."

The plane bumped and rocked above a sea of cloud. Although it was late in the morning, the sky was dark. A fork of lightning cracked downwards, flashing against the silver skin of the aircraft. The rain hurtled past it, forming curtains against the tiny windows. Inside, the lights had been dimmed. A soft, yellow glow illuminated the rows of passengers sitting in their seats, trapped inside the metal carcass. Nobody was talking. But as every buffet of wind made the plane shudder, as the tone of the engine rose and fell in the swirling air-pockets, eyes were raised heavenward, hands were clasped and tongues ran over dry lips.

Martin was going through a storm of a very different kind. Shortly after they had changed planes in Caracas he had fallen asleep and, in his sleep, he was revisiting a nightmare world that he knew too well.

Once again he found himself on a rugged tower of rock, surrounded by a bubbling, black ocean. Overhead, the clouds raced across a threatening sky. The wind howled around him, needles of salt water stinging his face. A short way off, four children stood on a bleak, rubble-strewn beach. Silently they looked up at him, their eyes fixed on him, pleading with him to join them. But he was trapped, alone on his rocky tower.

Then somehow, impossibly, one of the children had reached him. He found himself looking at a boy of his own age, felt the boy's hand on his shoulder, heard the boy call him by name. And he could see a way down from the rock. A staircase led to the beach. Eagerly he stepped forward.

There was an explosion of thunder. Martin looked upwards and screamed. A scorpion had appeared. A huge, golden scorpion, scuttling across the clouds towards him on eight squat legs. When it was directly above him, it stopped. Then it twisted round and its poisoned tail whipped down.

At the same moment, the surface of the ocean shattered. It was as if the water had become a mirror that had been smashed. Brilliant light burst out of the lines that had been formed, blinding him. Martin reached out for the boy who had been standing beside him only a moment ago but he was no longer there.

The scorpion's tail knifed into him. He reeled backwards. The rock crumbled away. And the world turned upside down as he fell, headlong into the night . . .

With a jolt, the plane touched down in Lima.

"Wake up," Richard Cole said. "We've arrived."

6
Lima

The passengers in the plane were standing up and reaching for their hand luggage as Martin blinked and unfastened his seat belt. His mouth was dry and his clothes felt like an old vegetable sack. He had been travelling for twenty-one hours. With the five-hour time change it was now twelve thirty exactly.

"Come on!" Richard said, handing him his case and pulling down another from the overhead locker. "You look awful."

"I had a nightmare," Martin said.

"So did I," Richard said. "It was called Flight VA 920 to Lima. But mercifully it's over. Let's get out."

The man who had boarded the plane at Caracas was very fast. One moment he was trying to brush past Richard, the next he seemed to trip, falling against the journalist's luggage. For just two seconds his hand was inside the bag. Then Richard was helping him to his feet while he was apologizing in rapid Spanish. Richard never felt the man's hand dart into his pocket. And although he noticed that his bag, which had been zipped up when he placed it on the seat, was now open, he didn't give it another thought. With a final apology, the man continued down the aisle. Then he was out of the plane and striding across the tarmac.

Richard and Martin reached the door a minute later. At once they were hit by a great wave of heat. It was unpleasant and sticky although there wasn't a cloud in the sky. The plane had docked next to a long, narrow building which ran down to a tall tower. All the airport buildings were painted a bright white, reflecting the sun until they were almost painful to look at.

Together they stepped out of the aeroplane and followed the other passengers across the tarmac to the entrance to passport control and customs. As they reached the door, Martin tapped at his pocket and groaned.

"My passport," he said. "I think it dropped out while I was asleep."

Richard looked back at the plane. "You'd better go back and get it. I'll wait for you here."

"No. You go ahead and queue for passport control. Otherwise we'll be at the end of the line. I'll catch you up."

Martin ran back to the plane. Even over such a short distance, the effort brought the sweat to his brow so great was the heat. He pushed past the last passengers and explained to the stewardess what he had come for. Then he made his way back to the seat. The passport wasn't there. He looked down the sides and underneath then behind the cushions. Soon he found he was alone on the plane except for a tired-looking stewardess who was staring at him angrily. Martin was beginning to panic. He had been on the plane for the best part of ten minutes but his passport seemed to have disappeared. As a last resort, he pulled open the luggage compartment. With a sigh of relief, he saw the missing passport, lying where it had fallen out of his hand luggage.

As he left the plane for a second time, he was surprised by the sound of whistling. Four armed soldiers ran across the tarmac and disappeared into the arrival lounge.

There seemed to be some sort of disturbance in the passport hall. Even from a distance he could hear the babble of voices raised in Spanish and he could see vague shapes—policemen, soldiers and other officials—milling about behind the windows. Anxious to rejoin Richard, Martin hurried forward, pulling his case along with him.

Although he had seen many terrible sights, the scene that greeted Martin inside the arrival lounge was in many ways the worst of all.

At the end of a wide corridor, Richard was being held against a wall, a gun pointing at his chest. There was a soldier on either side of him and two shirt-sleeved officials were shouting at him at the same time. The journalist's hand luggage was spread out on a table in front of him. One of the soldiers was holding four plastic bags in his hand. As Martin watched, a policeman put his hand into Richard's jacket pocket. When he pulled it out, he was holding two more plastic bags. The bags were transparent. They were filled with a white powder which looked like salt.

Now the other passengers were being hurried along the corridor by more shouting soldiers. Martin found himself being carried along with them and as he went he overheard snippets of conversation that came like fragments from a bad dream.

"He's an Englishman. Must be out of his mind . . ."

"Carries a life sentence, smuggling cocaine . . ."

"I understand somebody tipped them off . . ."

"I wouldn't like to be in his shoes . . ."

The stream of people continued down the corridor and out through another door. Martin fought against it, trying to reach his friend. He wanted to call out, but he would never have been heard above the din. He saw Richard trying to explain in broken Spanish; he saw one of the policemen produce a pair of handcuffs and slap them on the journalist's wrists. Then, suddenly, their eyes met. Richard saw Martin. Martin opened his mouth to call out. But Richard's eyes widened. He shook his head desperately. Martin hesitated. Once again, Richard shook his head, urging him on. And then he was gone and Martin was being pulled through a door, out into the passport control while Richard was bundled out under military escort through a door that was promptly locked behind him.

The whole incident had been witnessed by an old man, mopping the floor in the arrival hall. As Martin passed him, the old man froze. Then he dropped the mop and hurried away into a side office. Here, he found a telephone and with a trembling hand dialled a number. A minute later he was connected.

"Huascar?" he said. "The boy has come." He spoke in a language that was neither Spanish nor English. "He came with a friend, but there has been trouble." He paused as the voice at the other end of the line interrupted. "I'm certain it's him," he continued at last. "I felt his power. For a moment he stood next to me and I could feel it. The boy is Martin Hopkins. He is in Lima. And now he is alone."

Martin had never felt more on his own. Standing outside the airport, he tried to work out what had happened. Somebody had obviously known they were coming and had set a trap. Thanks to the lost passport he had escaped. But what could he do? He was carrying one change of clothes in his hand luggage, along with his camera and the guide book. He also had money, for Richard had given him fifty pounds to carry in case of emergency and he still had his passport. But how far would fifty pounds take him? He would just have to manage as best he could until Richard was freed.

There was nothing to be gained by staying at the airport. Martin had noticed a Bureau de Change and a ticket office for a coach into the city next to the main airport entrance. He approached them. Fortunately, the man at the Bureau de Change spoke good English and he was able to change ten pounds for a fistful of wrinkled, pink notes. The coach into Lima cost him one thousand Peruvian soles. As he handed over the money, he felt as if he was parting with a huge sum, though the cost was actually less than a pound.

Ten minutes later the coach arrived. It was an old, rusty, shuddering affair and only half-a-dozen other passengers had chosen it in preference to the taxis. They were spread out over the plastic seats, their luggage piled up next to the driver. Strangely enough, although he was young and obviously unaccompanied, nobody seemed to spare Martin a second glance. As the bus rumbled out of Lima airport, he felt a faint stirring of hope. Perhaps the next few days wouldn't be as difficult as he feared. Perhaps he might even be able to achieve something on his own.

From his window seat, he took in his first view of Lima. The road from the airport was a wide dual carriageway, bordered on both sides by a wasteland of dust and rubble. Huge posters advertising drinks like 7-Up and Inca Cola had been erected almost as if to hide the desolation. Here and there the coach passed clusters of shanty huts; small, square houses built of clay and corrugated iron. Children in ragged clothing scrabbled in the dust. Dogs, so thin that they looked like four-legged spiders, stood panting in the sun. In the distance, a mountain range, grey and hazy, loomed over them.

As the city drew nearer, the coach was hemmed in on all sides by dozens of taxis and buses that seemed to roar from all directions into noisy and hopelessly entangled traffic jams. The buses, filled to bursting, were painted a multitude of colours under the dust, giving them the appearance of something out of a decrepit circus. Everything in the city looked at least thirty years old.

Even the new factories and skyscrapers looked as though they were already decaying.

In the twenty minute journey, the sky grew darker, closing in and making the heat all the heavier. The coach turned into a wide square surrounded by shadowy arcades with a statue of a man on horseback in the centre and stopped. The driver called out something in Spanish. The doors hissed open. The journey was evidently over.

It was only when Martin had stepped onto the pavement and the hydraulic doors had closed behind him that the full enormity of his situation hit him. Since the plane had landed, he had allowed events to carry him forward. Now he was alone in the huge central square, traffic and pedestrians flowing all around him. All was noise and confusion. Overhead, the sun had vanished behind a grey haze. Enclosed by the towering buildings with not a sign in English to reassure him, he suddenly felt lost and afraid. He had nowhere to go.

With an effort, he pulled himself together. The first thing was to find a hotel. There was a hotel—The Bolivar—to his left, but one glance at the elegant facade and smart doorman told him that his fifty pounds would hardly last him a single night there. He opened his bag and found the guide book. There was a chapter devoted to hotels in Lima, each one graded for quality. He chose one with no star at all, found it on the map, picked up his bag and set off.

According to the guide-book, the big square was called the Plaza San Martin. He crossed it and went up a crowded walkway with modern shops and cinemas on both sides. Here everything was bright and cheerful, but as he turned off, following the map, the roads became quieter and narrower. Instead of shops there were only flats and offices with shuttered windows and blank, crumbling walls. Worse still, the names of the streets seemed to differ from the names in Richard's out-of-date guide book. He walked for ten minutes before he realized that he had absolutely no idea where he was.

Tired, hot and depressed, he was about to retrace his steps to the walkway when he saw two young men leaning against a wall, smoking cigarettes. Dragging his case (which seemed to have got heavier with every passing moment) he went over to them.

"Excuse me," he said. "Do you speak English?"

One of the men took his cigarette out from between his nicotine-stained teeth and nodded. "I speak a little."

"Do you know the Hotel Espinar in Union Street?"

The man looked at his friend, up and down the street, then back to Martin. "Yes. I know it well. But is far from here." He smiled. "We show you."

The three of them set off together back down the street, even further from the city centre. As they walked, the Peruvian chatted to Martin, smiling all the while.

"You are alone in Lima?" he asked.

"Yes."

"You come today?"

"Yes. By air from London." They turned down another street, this one even quieter and darker than the one before. "Is the hotel far?" Martin asked. He was beginning to feel uneasy in the company of the two Peruvians.

"No. No far. Two minutes from here."

They turned a corner and passed through a gateway. Martin just had time to register that far from leading him to a hotel, the two men had led him into a deserted car park. Then he was pushed forward, the bag flying from his hand. He called out, but there was nobody to hear him. The next moment they were on top of him. He tried to fight, but they were too strong. He felt his wallet being snatched out of his pocket, heard the men's laughter as they pulled out the money. He managed to get to his feet, only to be knocked down again as they turned their attention to his case. Out came the camera and the clothes. Martin sank back against the hard rubble. There was nothing he could do.

But they hadn't finished yet. Pouncing on him again, they tore off his wristwatch. Then they dragged his jacket off him, tearing his shirt. All these things were stuffed back into the case. Finally, laughing, they ran off, leaving Martin lying on his back in the empty car park.

After a time, he stood up and staggered over to the gate. There was a bench outside in the street and he sat down. Wrapping his arms around himself, he rocked silently, his eyes closed. He was still there when the sun set and the city prepared itself for the night.

7

Pedro

Martin opened his eyes. He had dozed off, sitting on the bench, but now somebody was tugging insistently at his sleeve. He looked down and saw a small, hairy hand, clutching the cuff of his shirt. His eyes went past the hand and followed the arm up until he found himself looking into the pink face of a baby marmoset. The monkey stared back with wide eyes. It was crouching beside him on the bench, its long, stripey tail hanging down to the ground. A minute later, a voice in the distance called out. "Charley!" The monkey chattered excitedly and pulled again at Martin's sleeve.

The street was still empty but two lamps had lit up. A figure appeared round a corner and walked towards the bench. It was a boy. As he drew closer, Martin saw that he was a Peruvian with olive skin, long, jet black hair cut in a fringe and dark brown eyes. He was exactly the same height and build as Martin and—Martin guessed—more or less the same age. In fact, but for a slightly thinner face and a slightly smaller nose, the Peruvian boy could have been a South American version of himself. He was dressed in ragged clothes; faded jeans and a torn, grey T-shirt. In that respect too they were similar, for Martin's own shirt had been almost ripped in half and he had gashed his trousers, along with his leg, when he had been attacked.

The boy stopped, facing the bench, and spoke. Martin could not tell whether he was addressing the monkey or himself for he spoke in rapid Spanish. The monkey, however, seemed to understand. It bounced off the bench, clambered across the pavement and leapt onto the boy, wrapping its hands around his neck and grinning. The boy spoke again, this time to Martin.

"I'm sorry," Martin said. "I don't speak Spanish."

"Are you American?" the boy asked, changing languages without blinking.

"No. I'm English."

"Are you OK?"

"No. I . . ." Martin shivered, remembering what he had been through.

The boy sat down beside him, looking at him curiously. "What happened?" he asked.

"Two men . . ." Martin took a deep breath. "They robbed me. They took everything I have." He felt in his pockets. "My money. My passport. My clothes. Everything."

The boy shook his head. "You were real lucky."

"Lucky?"

"Sure. They didn't kill you. That happens often here. Where are you staying?"

Martin sighed. "I don't have a hotel. I don't have anywhere to go. It's a long story . . ."

The two boys sat for a minute while the Peruvian took this in. "You've nowhere to go?" he repeated.

"I'm afraid not."

"And no friends?"

"No-one who can help me."

"Then you'd better come back with me. It sounds like you got plenty of problems."

"Do you live near here?" Martin asked.

"Sure. I got a place two blocks away."

"Won't your parents mind?"

The Peruvian boy shrugged. "There's no problem." He looked at Martin's leg, noticing the deep cut for the first time. "Can you walk on the leg?" he asked.

"I think so."

"Good. Let's go then."

They stood up, Martin leaning against the Peruvian boy for support. "What's your name?" he asked.

"Pedro." He smiled and gestured at the monkey which was still crouching on his shoulder. "And this is my monkey, Charley."

It took them twenty minutes to reach Pedro's house. They spoke little during the walk. Pedro didn't seem to be particularly interested in how Martin had come to find himself alone in the middle of Lima. He was more concerned about Charley who, it turned out, had escaped and run away that evening.

"I been looking for him all over," Pedro said. "I still don't know how he got out of the house. He's a bad monkey."

"Where exactly is your house?" Martin asked.

"Not far."

"Are your parents there?"

"You'll see."

They eventually reached a large building that was clearly on its last legs. The walls were propped up with heavy beams of wood and part of the roof had caved in. The windows were boarded over and a wire fence kept it well separated from the road. Large signs in red letters clearly warned trespassers to keep away.

Ignoring the signs, Pedro walked up to the fence and pushed. A whole section swung inwards. "This way," he said, helping Martin through. They crossed a strip of muddy, pitted ground and approached a door set between two wooden pillars. Pedro opened it. "My home," he announced, proudly.

The door led into a single, spacious room with two smaller rooms, one on either side. While Martin stood on the porch, Pedro produced a box of matches and proceeded to light about a dozen candles that stood on tables and on the arms of chairs around the room. As the light flickered and grew, Martin was able to take in his surroundings. The place was a slum, a derelict, forgotten house that should have fallen, or been knocked down years ago. However, Pedro had turned it into some sort of home. Besides the tables and chairs there were two cupboards, a chest of drawers and, strangely, an old piano. All the furniture was battered and broken and had obviously come off a rubbish tip, but Pedro had cleaned it and arranged it as though it were the very latest in good design. There were even pictures on the walls, hanging without glass in splintered frames. A colourless, threadbare carpet covered the floor. The whole place smelt of dust and damp.

"Sit down," Pedro said. Martin lowered himself into the sturdiest-looking chair.

"Are you hungry?"

"No thanks."

"That's good. There's no food here. I've eaten out tonight." Pedro twisted his shoulders and Charley sprang off to sit in one corner of the room, chuckling quietly.

"So this is where you live," Martin said.

"Sure. It's my place. What do you think?" Pedro gestured at the two doors, his every movement fast and jerky as though he were unable to control the energy inside him. "That's my bedroom in there. Charley has the other room. He's really messy. I'm always clearing up after him."

Martin looked through the doors. Through one he could see a bare mattress, stretched out on the floor. In the other room there was what looked like part of a table with a single drawer in the front.

"It's a nice place," Pedro said. "It's my home."

He reached into the cupboard and produced a bottle and two chipped glasses.

"Maybe you better have a drink," he said. He opened the bottle. "This is special. I don't have guests too often."

"What is it?" Martin asked.

"It's called Pisco. It's the national drink in Peru. I think it's a sort of brandy." Martin took his glass and sipped. The Pisco was bitter but it warmed him inside.

"Where did you get it?" he asked.

"I stole it."

They drained their glasses. Charley had curled up where he sat and gone to sleep. The candles flickered, making shadows dance on the walls.

"So, OK," Pedro said. "Who are you?"

"I'm Martin Hopkins."

"Martin. That's a good name. Like San Martin in Lima. So how come you have nowhere to go? Why are you in the city being robbed all by yourself? That's really . . . strange."

"Like I said, it's a long story. Why don't you tell me about yourself?"

Pedro nodded. "That's a long story too," he said. "I tell you what. I tell you all about me and then you tell me all about you and after that we get some sleep. OK?"

"Fine," Martin agreed.

Pedro unscrewed the bottle and poured two more glasses of Pisco. Then he sat down opposite Martin and stretched out his legs. "I am Pedro," he announced. Martin nodded. "I only have one name. I never knew my parents and I don't know what they were called. I think they died when I was a baby. I don't know.

"When I was a kid, I lived with a woman. I called her Aunt Maria, but I guess she wasn't really my aunt. She worked as a waitress in a posh restaurant. She used to bring me food back that people didn't want to eat. We used to have real good dinners then.

"Anyway, she started going out with this American

guy. Then he moved into the apartment. His name was Jack. He didn't work; just stayed in the place all day long. That's how I learn English. He taught me to read and write. Now I can read and write in English but my Spanish isn't so good. That's crazy. Well, Jack was a real bad man. He used to drink a lot and then he'd start hitting Aunt Maria and sometimes he hit me too. In the end, Aunt Maria disappeared. Maybe he killed her. I don't know. Well, a couple of days later, Jack ran off as well and then I was alone. I guess I was about nine then. It was four years ago.

"I was already working. I had a shoe-shine box. A lot of kids shine shoes out here. It's a real lousy job. Ten minutes' work for maybe a hundred soles. Ten pairs of shoes a day if you're lucky. I managed to get money out of the tourists because I speak English. But the big hotels didn't like to see me. They think I'm bad news. So I just had to do the shoe-shining and when I didn't have enough money, I stole food. I nearly got caught once or twice, but I can run pretty fast . . .

"I lived in Aunt Maria's place for time but in the end I had to go. After that I found places like this. There are plenty of them in Lima if you know where to look. This one is the best. It's dry and it's not too cold. I'm OK here. But I really hated the shoe-shining. I thought maybe I'd have to start stealing more, but then I found Charley.

"That was real lucky. He was on a rubbish heap. Somebody had thrown him out because he was dying. That monkey was in a real bad state. But I took him in and somehow—I don't know how—he got better. Maybe it's because he liked me. He got strong again and I called him Charley after a cartoon that Jack used to read."

Pedro got up and went into one of the rooms. A moment later he came back, pushing the strange contraption that Martin had seen. "I made this," he said. "I take it out in the street. Inside the drawer . . ." He opened it.

". . . there's all these little pieces of paper. I had to buy them. Charley tells people's fortunes. All the papers have messages on—you know, about money and love and all that stuff. I trained Charley to pick out one paper and give it to the tourist. I get 200 soles, sometimes 500 soles for that, and I do it maybe fifty times a day. That's good money. Now I can pay for food and candles and sometimes clothes. One day maybe I'll think of something else to do. I want to go to America so I can be rich. But it's OK for now."

He closed the drawer and sat down again. "So that's my story," he said. "Now, what about you?"

Pedro had told his tale with a face of such seriousness that although Martin had never heard anything quite like it, there could be no doubt he was telling the truth. So now he decided to tell the whole truth himself. While Pedro had talked, he had felt something digging into his thigh. Reaching into his back pocket, he had found the biro that he had picked up in Chelsea a few days (it seemed like a few years) before.

Now he laid it carefully on the table. "All right, Pedro," he began. "But I think I ought to warn you. Your English is terrific, but I think this is going to be pretty difficult to understand . . ."

Later that night, Martin woke up quite suddenly from a deep sleep. For a moment he wondered where he was. Then he remembered. He was lying on a spare mattress, covered by a thin blanket. He could make out the shape of Pedro who was lying on his own mattress a few yards away. He reached down to scratch his leg which was itching. His hand stopped. He sat bolt upright in the darkness.

He had limped to bed, the gash in his leg throbbing painfully. Now his hand was resting on the place where the wound had been. But it was gone. He rubbed his hand over his leg. The skin was smooth, unbroken. For a long time he sat still, deep in thought. Then he turned over and went back to sleep.

8
On the Ninth Floor

Martin was woken up late the next morning by the most extraordinary sound. It was music, but like no music he had ever heard before. Looking through the door he saw Pedro sitting at the piano, his face set with the concentration of a concert artist. He seemed to be playing a tango, but the instrument was so out-of-tune and missing so many notes that it was impossible to say quite what it was. Charley was sitting on the top of the piano with his eyes closed and his hands clamped over his ears. Pedro's tune reached a crescendo and with a last, jangling chord he stopped. Inside the piano there was a twang as a string snapped. Martin stretched and got out of bed.

"*Buenos días*," Pedro said, seeing him. Charley opened his eyes and grinned. "How are you feeling?"

"I'm fine." Martin walked into the room. "Except that all my clothes are ruined."

"Here." Pedro handed him a pile of old clothes. "These are mine. I think maybe they fit."

"Thanks."

"Do you want breakfast?"

"I'm starving." Martin pulled on a pair of Pedro's

trousers. They fitted him perfectly. "Do you have a kitchen here?"

"No kitchen, no bathroom, no toilet. Come on. We'll go out."

The two boys walked back towards the centre of Lima, leaving Charley locked up in the house. It was a brighter day although the air was still close and damp, but as Pedro explained, it was always like that in the city. At last they arrived at a bus station outside which were a number of stalls and benches set up on the pavement. The smell of sweet tea and fried eggs, cooking out in the open, filled the air. They sat down at one of the stalls and Pedro ordered tea and two sandwiches. The owner, an old, toothless, woman, smiled at him as if she knew him well.

"This is really good, Pedro," Martin said as he ate. The egg was cold and greasy but he was so hungry he didn't care.

"OK Martin. But here's the question. What are you going to do?"

Martin sighed. "I don't know. I've got to help Richard somehow. I suppose I'll have to go to the Embassy . . . "

"No. That's a real bad idea." Pedro frowned. "You go to the Embassy, they just hold onto you or hand you over to the police like your friend. Maybe it takes three weeks before they let you go."

"What other choice do I have?"

Pedro sipped tea from his tin mug. "Let me see if I get you right," he said. "There are creatures—the Old Ones. They're bad, but they're in another world. But you think they're going to break into Peru, right? You don't know where. You don't know when. But you think it's happening soon."

"That's about it."

"OK. You say you've got some sort of magic power. That sounds pretty crazy to me. But you don't look crazy so I believe you. So you've got to find these Old Ones so you can knock them out and then you go back to England and everything's OK. Right?"

"Right."

Pedro nodded. "So Charley and I have decided to help you." He raised a hand as Martin began to protest. "You can't do anything by yourself," he said. "You have to money. You don't speak the language. I think you last maybe ten minutes by yourself."

"But it might be dangerous."

"Dangerous? Everything's dangerous. But Charley and me, we're dangerous too. You'll see."

They finished their meal and Pedro paid. Martin noticed that his new friend only had a handful of coins in his pocket. "Look, Pedro," he said. "One day I'll be able to pay you back. But right now we need money."

"Sure." Pedro smiled. "So we'll get some money."

"How?"

A bus had drawn into the station full of passengers just back from a morning excursion. The doors opened and they began to climb out, carrying coats and bags. Pedro eyed them up carefully before speaking again. "You see that man?" He pointed to a fat Englishman in a brightly coloured shirt who was mopping his brow while his wife struggled with their luggage.

"Yes," Martin said.

"Go and talk to him."

Martin had a good idea what Pedro had in mind. Biting his lip, he stepped forward and addressed the man. "Excuse me," he said.

"Yes?" The Englishman threw his jacket over his shoulder, sweating.

"Er . . . do you know if there's a bus to . . . er . . . San Martino?" Martin asked.

"San Martino?" The man scowled. "I've never even heard of it."

"Well, it's a little town . . ." Out of the corner of his eye, Martin saw Pedro sidle up to the Englishman, his hand reaching out for the jacket. Afraid that the man would turn round, Martin said the first thing that came into his head. "It's famous for its prunes," he said.

"Prunes?" The Englishman looked at him as though he were mad.

"Yes. Peru prunes. They're particularly good."

The man grunted. "Stop wasting my time," he said, walking off.

Martin joined Pedro who was on the other side of the street by now. "Did you do it?" he asked.

"Sure. You make a good crook." Pedro took his hand from behind his back. He was holding a thick, black wallet. He flicked it open. There was about a hundred pounds in cash inside, along with an American Express card.

Martin took it. "That'll do nicely," he said.

They stopped again three blocks away. "All right," Pedro said. "We have money. Lots of money. So what do you want to do next?"

"TC, Lima," Martin replied. "Whatever that is, we've got to find it. It's the one clue we have."

"I thought so too," Pedro nodded. "That's why I bring us here."

"What do you mean?"

Pedro turned round and pointed. "TC, Lima," he repeated. "We're standing in front of it."

It was a nine-storey building, modern and unwelcoming. On the roof was a bright yellow cube, revolving, with a clock on one side and the two letters TC in red on the other. Beside the door was a bronze plaque reading *Tovar Communications Ltd. (Lima)*.

"Who is Tovar?" Martin asked.

"He's one of the richest men in Peru," Pedro told him. "Really loaded. His company makes computers and all that stuff. This is their HQ, but they've got a big . . . I don't know the word . . . sort of scientific place in the south, in Paracas."

"Well, this must be where the biro came from," Martin said.

"So what are you going to do, Martin?"

"Give me the wallet. I think I've got an idea."

With Pedro behind him, he walked straight into the office building. There was a reception desk inside the door and they were stopped by a young woman.

"Do you speak English?" Martin asked.

"Yes," she replied. "What do you want?"

"I was wondering if a Mr. Todd worked here."

"Why do you want to know?"

Martin held up the wallet. "I found this on the street," he explained. "It had this address on it."

The receptionist became more friendly. "You're very honest," she said. "If you leave it with me . . ."

"Can't we give it to him ourselves?" Martin gave her a hopeful smile, the smile of a poor boy hoping for a reward.

She understood and smiled back. "Mr. Todd is on the ninth floor with Signor Valenzuela de Tovar," she said. "I can't disturb him now." She gestured towards some leather sofas. "But if you'd like to wait, he should be down in ten minutes or so."

Martin and Pedro sat down on a sofa. They waited until the doors opened again and a man carrying a pile of parcels walked in.

"Now!" Martin whispered.

While the receptionist's attention was diverted, they slipped off the sofa and made their way down the first corridor they saw. After about twenty yards they came to a set of lifts. Martin went straight past them, searching for a doorway. He found one and opened it. As he had hoped, it led to a staircase.

"Where are we going?" Pedro asked.

"Up," Martin said.

"Can't we take the elevator?"

"The lift?" Martin shook his head. "We might be seen. Anyway, it's only nine floors."

65

"It's not that, Martin," Pedro said. "It's just that I've never been in an elevator before."

"Maybe on the way down."

They climbed up to the ninth floor. It was one o'clock and the office was quiet with most of the staff out at lunch. Nobody challenged them as they made their way down a long corridor with framed photographs of the planets between each door. There was a single door at the end of the corridor, different from the others in that it seemed to have been constructed for a child. It was at least a foot shorter than any other door on the floor. And it was slightly ajar. Martin stopped and listened. Inside the room, two men were talking in Spanish. He motioned to Pedro who took his place.

". . . but we must move quickly," a voice was saying.

"How long will Chambers be gone?" This voice belonged to Mr. Todd.

"At least two days, perhaps longer. And by the time the professor gets back, the search will be over."

"Why do we even need to look?" Mr. Todd asked. "You have the book."

"We have to be sure." The voice of Victor Valenzuela de Tovar was cold and determined. "The positioning of the golden scorpion must be precise. The precise moment. The precise place. If Chambers . . ."

He stopped as the phone rang. "I said I didn't want to be disturbed!" he snapped. There was a pause. "What boys?" Another pause, then he addressed Todd. "Have you lost your wallet?"

"No."

"But . . ." He spoke again into the telephone. "They are not to leave the building on any account. Inform the guards. They are to shoot to kill if necessary."

"Let's move," Pedro whispered. "I think we got trouble."

They hurried away. About half way along the corridor, between two photographs of the Earth taken from outer space, there was another open door, this one leading into what turned out to be a large store-room. Even as they swung the door shut behind them, Todd and Tovar strode out of the office.

"There's nobody here," the German said.

"They were here. I know they were here."

"Who?"

"The English boy, Hopkins—and someone else. Find them, Mr. Todd. They must be somewhere near."

In the store-room, Pedro heard Tovar's command. "They're coming!" he whispered. Martin looked around him. Apart from a row of shelves and a photo-copying machine, there was nothing in the room, nowhere to hide. At the far end, there was a window. Quickly, he went over to it and slid it open. "This way!" he whispered.

Pedro was standing beside the photo-copier. "Martin . . ." he began.

"No time. We've got to get out of here."

Thirty seconds later, the door opened and Mr. Todd walked in. He looked around him.

"Not here," he said.

"The window?" Tovar asked.

"We're nine floors up. They must be in one of the other rooms."

"Find them, Todd. That boy must be stopped."

As Todd was examining the store-room, Martin and Pedro were pressed against the side of the building, clinging to it with their finger-nails. A ledge, no more than six inches wide, ran around the side of the office. Awkwardly, they shuffled along, feeling the empty air beneath their heels. Nine floors beneath them, the sun glared off a hard, white pavement.

But less than twenty yards away, a fire-escape zig-zagged down to the ground. This was what Martin had seen. Carefully, one step at a time, his stomach scraping against the wall, he was making for it, Pedro a little way behind. He dared not look down, afraid that he would become dizzy. With his eyes half-closed, his heart pounding, he edged sideways. Every inch seemed to take an hour. Then, at last, his hand closed on the cold iron of the rail. At that moment, Pedro fell.

The Peruvian boy had been trying to catch up. He had taken a large step and his shirt had caught on the rough corner of a broken brick. Pulling free, he had lost his balance. Teetering on the edge, he gave a yell and pitched backwards into the void. Martin lunged forward, one hand stretched out. Somehow he managed to grab hold of Pedro. For a moment the two of them hung there while Pedro scrabbled at nothing as he tried to find a new foothold. Martin pulled upwards with all his strength. He fell back onto the fire-escape platform. Pedro came with him. They were safe.

Not for long, however. Mr. Todd had heard Pedro's shout and as the two boys began to hurtle down the fire-escape he drew a gun and, leaning out of the window, fired. The bullet clanged off the metal staircase just a few feet above them.

They reached the bottom and paused. They were in a narrow alley leading to the main street. For a moment, Martin thought they were lucky since there wasn't another person in sight. But then a door opened and a uniformed guard stepped out, his hand reaching for his holster. Martin looked back the other way. The alley led to a high brick wall. There was no other way out. His heart sank as the security man approached.

Suddenly there was a screech of tyres. A car twisted off the street and began to speed towards them. The security officer half turned, just in time to throw himself out of the way as the car roared past him. Martin and Pedro prepared to do the same. It seemed that the driver was intent on running them down, but at the last moment he stopped. "Get in!" a voice commanded in English.

Martin looked at Pedro, then up at the fire-escape.

Mr. Todd was already half way down, his gun in his hand. Inside the building, an alarm bell had begun to ring. Two more security men appeared at the top of the alley. Without another word, the two boys threw themselves into the car. At once the driver reversed up the alley. "Keep down!" he shouted. A second later there was a shot and a side window frosted. The car lurched to one side, sending a dustbin flying. But then the driver spun the wheel and the car leapt over the pavement and shot out into the traffic. They were away.

Nobody spoke as they raced out of the centre of Lima, making for the suburbs. Crouching in the back seat, neither of the boys could see their rescuer, but Martin found himself wondering if he had ever driven before. The car was weaving about the road as if out of control. And they had scarcely gone half a mile before it suddenly mounted the pavement for a second time and came to a halt in a mass of bushes.

Martin was the first to recover. Pushing open the door, he got out and staggered round to the front of the car. He looked at the driver, a young Indian man he had never seen before. Now he understood why their journey had been so short. The man had been hit by a bullet in the side of the neck. He was slumped over the wheel, blood soaking his shirt and jacket. His eyes, however, were still open. Taking a deep breath, he spoke.

"Go . . . to Cuzco." He coughed and swallowed with difficulty. "On Friday . . . the temple of Coricancha. In Cuzco . . . at six o'clock. You must . . ." Then blood curtained over his lip and his eyes closed.

"Who is he?" Pedro asked, standing beside Martin.

"I don't know. He spoke English, but he must be Peruvian."

"I think we better move, Martin."

"But . . ."

"Come on!" Pedro pulled him away. Already a small crowd had formed round the car and they could hear police cars approaching. They forced their way through the people and headed off down the first side-street.

"I should never have come," Martin muttered as they walked quickly away. "Richard's in prison. I nearly got you killed. I've managed to kill someone I've never even met. And what have I got? Nothing. Richard was right. The whole idea was crazy."

"It's not your fault, Martin," Pedro said. "And it's not true. I found something. I wanted to tell you, but you were in a hurry." He pulled a crumpled sheet of paper out of his pocket. "I found it in the photo . . . thing. It was in the tray. I think maybe it's a page out of the monk's diary."

9
Across Peru

"I will tell you a story," Victor Valenzuela de Tovar said.

He was sitting opposite Mr. Todd at a table that was a little shorter than all the other tables in one of Lima's smartest restaurants. The two men had just finished a meal of cebiche—raw fish and onions—which was the restaurant's speciality. It was the day after the break-in, but in those twenty-four hours he seemed to have aged. His body had deflated like a punctured balloon and his voice hissed softly, the sound of escaping air.

"Once, thousands of years ago, the world was ruled by creatures of immense power. Everything that lived bowed to them. Those that did not, died. The creatures came to be known by many names: devils, demons, furies, banshees . . . but originally they were called the Old Ones, the first great force of evil.

"However, by a trick, the Old Ones were cast out of this world and into an eternal darkness. You could say that this was the time when civilisation began. Civilisation? Look around you, Mr. Todd. The world is being torn apart by warfare and chaos. Pollution, famine, crime . . . every day our newspapers are filled with the glories of our so-called civilisation.

"For thousands of years, there have been those who believe that the world would be a better place were the Old Ones to return. They have been feared as black magicians, burnt as witches, hated and envied for their powers. They are the servants of the Old Ones, Mr. Todd, and I am one of them as my father was before me. Our secrets have been handed down from generation to generation and all our lives we have been working for one purpose: to bring the Old Ones back, to restore them to their rightful place and to begin a new age.

"It can be done. When the Old Ones were expelled from the world, two gates were created, two barriers between the finite and the infinite. One was in England. The other is here in Peru. I have known of the Peruvian gate for more than twenty years, but it was only when the diary was finally discovered that I realized I had the key to unlock it. The golden scorpion is that key. In just eleven days from now it will be in position. And then the new age will begin.

"But there is a danger. The Old Ones have enemies. Five defeated them at the dawn of time and five shall rise up against them again. The boy, Hopkins, is one of the five. He must not be allowed to remain alive. He has power. It is still growing in him and every second he lives it becomes stronger. When he was in my office building, I could feel it. It was . . . painful.

"But despite everything, he is still a child. Although he escaped me at Lima airport, he was seen by one of my agents only a few hours ago. He has left the city, by air. He and a Peruvian boy flew to Cuzco. I have no idea what they hope to find there, but whatever it is, they must be stopped."

Tovar pulled out an air-ticket and passed it across the table. "You will fly to Cuzco on the evening plane, Mr.

Todd," he said. "You will track down Martin Hopkins for me. And then you will kill him."

"So what does it mean?" Martin asked.

"I translated it," Pedro replied.

"I know. I know what it means, but I don't know what it means—if you know what I mean," Martin said.

"No," Pedro muttered.

As Tovar and Todd talked, the two boys were twenty thousand feet above the Andes, nearing Cuzco. Charley was on Pedro's lap, firmly secured in a basket cage they had bought that morning. Neither Pedro nor his monkey had ever flown before. Though terrified to begin with, they were now enjoying the flight, although Pedro was disappointed that they weren't allowed to open the windows.

Martin was examining the photo-copy that Pedro had found. Only part of the page was visible. Obviously, whoever had made the copy from the diary had put in the paper crookedly with the result that most of the image was no more than a blur. The part that remained was clear enough—except that as far as Martin could see, it was completely meaningless.

A number of straight lines had been drawn on the page, half of them lost in the smudged area, the rest forming no obvious pattern or shape. Beneath these, handwritten in Old Spanish, were four lines of verse which Pedro had translated:

> *On the night of the Scorpion*
> *Before the place of Qolqa,*
> *There will the light be seen*
> *The light that is the end of all light.*

Finally, beneath the poem, the same hand had written the words *Inti Raymi*. The two small i's had been dotted with miniature suns; one white, one black.

"What's the place of Qolqa?' Martin asked.

"I've never heard of it," Pedro said.

"Did you hear Tovar and Todd talking about it?"

Pedro cast his mind back to the office. "I'm sorry, Martin," he said. "It all happened so fast. All I remember is the name Chambers. They were afraid of a professor called Chambers. And there was something else . . . something about a gold scorpion."

"What about Inti Raymi?"

"I have heard those words," Pedro said. "But right now . . . I don't remember it."

"Perhaps it'll come to you."

Martin folded up the paper and put it back in his pocket. The *no smoking* lights came on and the plane lurched in the air. Pedro's hands seized the arms of his chair as they began their descent.

"I just wish I knew who the man in the car was," Martin said. "What are we meant to find in the Temple of Coricancha?"

"We don't know until we get there," Pedro said.

"I know. But how do we know that he was really on our side? For all we know it could be a trap." Martin sighed. "If only Richard was here."

"What's Richard like?" Pedro asked.

"He's hopeless. He hates flying and he's no good at adventures. If he'd had his way, I'd never have come here in the first place."

"Then maybe he couldn't help us," Pedro said.

"You're probably right. But he's my friend—and it's my fault he's in trouble. I just wish he was here, that's all." Martin fastened his seat belt and settled back in the seat. "I wonder what's happening to him now?" he said.

The man from the embassy drew up a chair to the plain, wooden table and sat down.

"I'm very sorry, Mr. Cole," he began.

"*You're* sorry?" Richard ran a hand through his be-draggled hair. "You've taken your time getting here," he complained. "It's been two days since I was arrested because of a ridiculous misunderstanding."

"That ridiculous misunderstanding was a kilogram of pure cocaine in your luggage, Mr. Cole," the man from the embassy reminded him.

"It was planted there."

"So you say But by whom? And why?"

"I wish I knew."

The man from the embassy, who had introduced himself as a Mr. Knights, opened his briefcase. "I trust you are not too uncomfortable here."

"Uncomfortable?" Richard laughed. "I haven't had a bath for two days. I'm in a cell the size of a broom-cupboard. And I don't even have it to myself. I'm sharing it with a man who murdered five priests during Mass. A mass-murderer, for Heaven's sake! And you ask me if I'm comfortable? I demand to see a lawyer."

"I am a lawyer," Mr. Knights said. "And I have to advise you, Mr. Cole, you are in very serious trouble."

Richard sank his head into his hands. "Who exactly are you?" he demanded.

"I told you . . ." Mr. Knights began.

"You're from the British Embassy. So why haven't you got me out of here. Whose side are you meant to be on?"

"It's a delicate situation." Mr. Knights coughed delicately. "If you are what you say you are, then of course I will do everything I can to get you freed. If, on the other hand, you are involved in certain . . . illegal activities . . . then it is in the British interest to help our Peruvian friends as much as possible."

"But I've told you . . ."

". . . the truth?" This time Mr. Knights interrupted. He shook his head and brought out a sheaf of papers. "I have your statement here," he went on. "But tell me,

Mr. Cole, why do you insist that you travelled to Peru alone . . ."Richard squirmed in his chair. ". . . when we know that you came in the company of a thirteen-year-old boy, a certain Martin Hopkins? Why did you come to Peru, Mr. Cole?"

"I said. It was a holiday."

"Then why did some mysterious Peruvian master-criminal try to frame you for cocaine smuggling?"

"I don't know. Perhaps he had a thing against tourists."

Mr. Knights shook his head. "It won't do, Mr. Cole. Listen. We know that you and the Hopkins boy were involved in that curious business at Forrest Hill. I have also received a report—a top secret report—that connects you with certain even more curious events in Yorkshire last April. And it would seem that even in the short time that Master Hopkins has been here, he has managed to involve himself in some still more curious affairs.

"According to reports we have received, he and another boy, a Peruvian of the same age, broke into the office of one of the country's most important businessmen. They were assisted in their escape by a third party, another Peruvian whose identity has not yet been established. This man managed to get himself shot and now Martin Hopkins has disappeared."

"How do you know it was Martin?" Richard asked.

"We don't for certain. The description, however, fits. And personally I rather doubt that there is more than one thirteen-year-old English boy loose on the streets of Lima.

"Let me be honest with you, Mr. Cole." The man from the embassy smiled. "The Ministry of Foreign Affairs has been taking the closest interest in your little escapades. The Minister himself is involved. He wants to know what you're up to. There are many questions we want answered. Now, you need our help. We can persuade the Peruvian authorities that you were, as you say, framed. But first you will have to co-operate." The smile froze. "Tell me what I want to know, Mr. Cole, or you're going to be here for an awfully long time."

The old man had listened carefully, his eyes half-closed, his head nodding in silent agreement. The messenger who had brought him the news sat down on the hard rock and waited for him to speak. Two more men stood nearby. Their faces were grim, but they dared not voice their doubts.

It was mid-day and the sun was burning, but the old man hardly noticed it. At last he spoke.

"Huascar told them where to find us before he died," he said.

"We think so," the messenger said. "They took a plane to Cuzco this morning. They are in the city now."

"Where?"

The messenger shook his head. "We don't know. The boys are afraid. I had them followed from the airport but they shook off the tail. However, it won't take us long to find them again."

"And the Peruvian boy? There can be no doubts who he is?"

"No doubt."

The old man smiled. It was a smile tinged with sadness, but there could be no mistaking the excitement in his voice. "Huascar did not die for nothing," he said. "In just a few days we will have them. Tomac!" One of the men looked up. "The time has come for the great congregation. Spread the word. Our city must be closed off in preparation. You know what to do."

"I know what to do," Tomac repeated.

"The boys will come to us on Friday, 19th June. We will meet on Saturday. Spread the word, Tomac," he commanded. "The day has at last arrived."

10

The Holy City

The fat Englishman mopped the back of his neck with a bright, spotted handkerchief and scowled.

"What do you mean there are no trains?" his wife demanded.

"That's what the fellow says, Shirley. Apparently there's been a landslide in the mountains. The line to Machu Picchu isn't running. The hotel is closed. You're not even allowed to walk there."

"But it's preposterous, Roger. We came all this way just to see it."

"Well I can't argue with him. He doesn't even speak English." He stuffed the handkerchief back into his pocket. "Some holiday this has turned out to be. First I lose my wallet in Lima. And now the biggest sight in Peru is closed."

As the English tourists walked out of Santa Ana, Cuzco's central station, they didn't notice a curious trio sitting on the steps outside. Martin and Pedro were finishing a late lunch of fruit and cheese which they had just bought at a stall. Between them, and attached to Pedro by a strong cord, Charley was munching a banana.

This was their third day in Cuzco, but it was the first time they had been far from the hotel. Almost as soon as they had arrived, they had both fallen ill. At 11,000 feet above sea-level, the air in the town was thin and the slightest exertion brought headaches and dizziness. They had only felt better after a day in bed.

But this wasn't the only reason why they had stayed indoors. Martin felt uneasy in the town. He had spotted the man at the airport almost at once. He had been in the taxi behind them as they drove into Cuzco. Eventually they had lost the man in the crowds, but now Martin couldn't take a step without feeling that they were being watched. He regretted having come to Cuzco at all, but it was too late. Friday had arrived. They had found the Temple of Coricancha in a guide book they had bought. In just two hours' time they would keep their mysterious appointment.

Now they sat quietly, finishing their meal. Outside the station there were dozens of tiny stalls selling fruit and vegetables, brushes and combs, clothes and shoes, knives and forks . . . a thousand different things. The ground was littered with paper and peelings and the air was thick with the smell of cooked meat. A great crowd of brightly dressed Indians—the women with bowler hats and pig-tails— bustled all around them.

"What are we going to do?" Pedro asked.

Martin looked at his guide book. "There's tons of stuff to see in Cuzco," he said. He read out loud. "Cuzco was once the capital of the Inca Empire. The 'four quarters of the Earth' as it was then called, must have been a magnificent place, perched on the edge of a valley high up in the Andes. Once it was a holy city, its great squares surrounded by gorgeous temples and palaces. In 1533, however, after the conquest by Pizarro and the Spaniards, it was almost completely burnt to the ground. Even so, much Inca stonework can still be seen today and there are many beautiful churches.

"A good tour of Cuzco will begin in the central square, the *Plaza de Armas*, where you will see . . ."

"Wait a minute, Martin," Pedro interrupted.

Martin lowered the book. "What's up?"

"Look." Pedro pointed. "We got trouble again."

Mr. Todd had spent two days tracking down Martin and Pedro. He had visited hotels, looked in shops and restaurants and asked at the tourist office. Then he had taken to the streets. Cuzco was a large town, but not that large. Now he stopped on the steps of a tall, bulky church at the top of the street, a smile tugging at his blank face. He was not alone. Four Indians with dark faces and narrow, unfriendly eyes stood with him, waiting like ragged vultures.

Pedro glanced at Martin. "Mr. Todd?" he asked.

Martin nodded.

"He's got no eyebrows."

"I've noticed."

"What do you think they want?"

"I don't know for sure," Martin said. "But I've got a nasty idea."

"Me too."

Charley whimpered and dropped his banana skin. Pedro pulled him closer and the monkey clambered onto his shoulder.

"Surely he can't do anything out in the street in broad daylight," Martin muttered.

"You want to wait and find out?" Pedro asked.

"What do you think?"

"I think we better move."

"I think you're right."

As one they darted across the road, weaving in and out of the stalls. Mr. Todd's face grew dark with anger; he spat out a command in Spanish. At once the four Indians moved forward.

Martin and Pedro, with Charley clinging to his neck, reached the other side of the road and plunged into the

main market of Cuzco underneath a wide tin roof. Here
there were so many stalls and so many people that it was
difficult to move.

"This way!" Martin cried, elbowing his way down a
narrow passage. Whole carcasses of lamb hung grey and
glistening over stone slabs and old Indian men watched
them curiously over flaking piles of dried meat. Sacks of
leaves and powders sprung up in front of them. They
ducked down a passage, through a gate and out into one
street, down another and on towards the centre of Cuzco.
Everywhere there were crowds of people. But nobody
paid them any attention.

Almost before they knew it, Martin and Pedro had
reached the *Plaza de Armas* with its huge cathedral, the
colour of dried blood, basking in the last of the sunlight.
In the centre of the square beside a fountain, they drew
to a halt.

"We must have lost them," Martin said, panting. With
the thin air, running was impossible for long. He could
feel his heart hammering in his chest as though it were
trying to break out.

"I wish you were right," Pedro gasped. He pointed.
Mr. Todd and his men had appeared on the far side of
the square. Even now they were moving slowly forward,
searching for them.

Martin looked round the square. There was nowhere
they could hide, but there were still plenty of people
around.

"We've got to be safe here," he said. "They can't do
anything with so many witnesses."

"*Madre Dios*, Martin!" Pedro cried. "This is Peru, not
England. Out here anything can happen. And it often
does."

They chose a steep, cobbled street that ran uphill next
to the cathedral and made for it. Powdery walls with
barred windows loomed up on both sides, the sloping
tiles of the roofs jutting forward and almost blocking

out the light. The street twisted to the right, then emerged in a wide, empty square. Martin stopped, straining for breath.

"I can't go on!" he sobbed.

"Got to . . ." Pedro wheezed. "Look . . ."

Mr. Todd was only twenty yards behind them and he was moving faster now. The Indians were fanning out across the square. Two of them had produced flick knives. All of them were smiling. The uphill run and the lack of oxygen seemed to have had no effect on them.

"We've got to find crowds," Martin said. "We're safer with people."

Pedro drew Charley closer to him. The monkey seemed to be aware of their danger, for his hands were pressed tight around Pedro's throat, almost throttling him. "This way!" Pedro said.

They ran down a long, gloomy alley and out into a wider street. There were fewer people in this part of the town, but seeing a small crowd, they made for it. It was a party of American tourists, grouped around a guide who was pointing at a wall and lecturing them enthusiastically. "This is the most famous wall in Cuzco," he was saying. "Each stone fits perfectly with no cement or anything. In fact they fit so perfectly that you can't even slip a razor blade between them. The stone that I'm pointing to has no less than twelve sides. I'm sure you'll all agree that this is a masterpiece of building . . ."

Martin and Pedro fell in with the tourists while they took photographs. Behind them, Mr. Todd and the Indians slowed down and stopped, the knives temporarily concealed. It was stalemate. But then the guide had finished his lecture and the tourists were queuing up to get into a waiting coach. Martin and Pedro moved forward with them.

"I'm very sorry," the guide said, stopping them. "This is a private coach."

"Listen," Martin said. "We're in trouble. Can you give us a lift?"

The guide looked at the two boys distastefully. "I'm afraid if you're not with Tompkins Tours," he said firmly, "you can't come in the coach."

"But somebody is trying to kill us."

"Not on a Tompkins Tour, they're not."

"Thanks a million," Martin muttered as the coach door hissed shut.

Taking a deep breath, they ran; round a corner and once more downhill. Already the shadows were growing as evening approached. With legs that hardly seemed to obey them, they lurched into another street, swerving onto the pavement to avoid a taxi that roared past them, horn blaring.

Then they were in another square, empty but for two old women crouching on the pavement beside a sweets stall.

"Which way?" Pedro gasped.

"There!" Martin pointed to the right.

"But Martin, that's up . . ."

"I know." Martin wiped his forehead. "But . . . I can't explain. We've just got to go that way."

Mr. Todd and the Indians reached the square a few moments later. They hesitated for only a second before they spotted the two boys, stumbling uphill as though they were running in slow motion.

"We have them," he muttered.

The five of them turned right and followed.

Martin could go no farther. They had to find somewhere to hide, to wait until the German had gone. He looked around him. To one side there was an open doorway leading into the dark interior of a church. Making an instant decision, he crossed the road and ran in, Pedro close behind.

It was only then that he realized where he was. They had intended to come here in less than an hour's time.

For this was Cor'c'icancha, the Court of Gold, once the most fabulous building in the Inca Empire.

Four thousand priests had once lived there, surrounded by gold. Then the Spanish had come. They had torn down everything they could lay their hands on, seizing the precious metal only to melt it down. On the ruins of the temple they had built a dull, ugly church. Now, as Martin paused breathless, he found himself on the edge of a barren courtyard. On both sides, protected under glass, were lines of Inca walls—all that remained of the old temple.

A corridor ran past one of the walls, leading to a door that seemed to open onto an outer terrace. Martin made for it, hoping to find a safe way out behind the church. After that, he would make his way back to the hotel. Only behind locked doors would he feel safe. Any thought of his mysterious rendezvous in the temple had gone out of his mind.

But his luck had run out. On one side the terrace was blocked off by a steel fence. On the other it turned a sharp corner and came to a dead end between three solid Inca walls. They were too high to jump down to the street. If Mr. Todd found them there, they would be trapped.

"Where now?" Pedro asked.

"Back," Martin said. "There must be another way out."

Hastily, he returned to the door, only to come to a halt, his heart sinking. The German was in the corridor. The Indians were with him. And at the same moment, they saw him. Slowly now, knowing that they had the boys cornered, they approached. Once again the cruel smile tugged at Mr. Todd's face.

"*Amigos!*"

Martin turned. A man had appeared from nowhere, walking along the terrace towards them. He was dressed in a bright, striped poncho with a woollen helmet covering his hair, ears and neck. Where had he come from? There was no way down from the terrace. And nor was there any way up.

"*Amigos*," the man repeated. "Come quickly."

"What's '*amigos*'?" Martin whispered.

"It means 'friends'," Pedro said.

"I wonder," Martin muttered.

But there was no time to think. Mr. Todd was only a few yards away. Martin and Pedro followed the stranger back along the terrace, turned the corner—and understood. Part of the wall had swung open, revealing a secret door. It was incredible. There was a passage inside the wall, concealed by stones that fitted so exactly that nobody would have suspected its existence. In the slanting sunlight, Martin could make out a staircase leading down, underneath the temple. Their rescuer had already entered the wall and was waiting for them. Taking a deep breath, the two boys stepped inside.

The wall swung shut behind them and the blackness smothered them up.

II

Under the Mountains

"They have to be here. They cannot have escaped me!"

Martin stood still in the darkness, scarcely daring to breath. He could hear every word Mr. Todd spoke as if they were standing next to one another. Indeed, he realized, that was just what they were doing. Nine inches of stone separated them. If they could have reached through it, they would have touched each other.

On the terrace, Mr. Todd was rigid with anger, but his disfigured face remained blank, unable to bend itself to emotion. The four Indians were searching everywhere without success. It seemed that the two boys had just vanished into thin air. At last they left. The sun sank behind Cuzco and the soft light of the evening washed over the city.

Inside the wall, Martin, Pedro and the stranger waited five minutes. Then the man produced a torch and flicked it on. Once again Martin saw the flight of steps leading down in the middle of the wall.

"Come," the man said. "But be careful. No fall."

"Who are you?" Martin asked.

"My name is Tomac. Now come."

It was a tight squeeze. As they went farther and farther

down, Martin could feel the weight of the stones pressing in on him. All was black. The torch was only powerful enough to light one or two steps ahead. The air became damp and cold. The staircase seemed to go on for ever. Martin had no idea where they were being led and he was beginning to wonder if this wasn't some even more dangerous trap when Tomac stopped and placed a hand on his arm. They had reached the bottom.

Tomac swung the torch and Martin was able to make out a small, circular cavern with three passages leading out.

"You stay close," Tomac said. "If you get lost down here, you die."

Martin and Pedro needed no further prompting. They entered a labyrinth of underground tunnels twisting left and right with fresh paths at every corner. Left alone for ten seconds, they would have got hopelessly lost, but their Indian guide never hesitated. The tunnels seemed to be unguarded. But, Martin guessed, any strangers trying to pass through the maze would wonder aimlessly until they died of starvation.

After about half an hour they paused. They must have been hundreds of feet underground, but to Martin's astonishment he could see light ahead. He moved on, Pedro next to him, leading Charley on his tether.

"What do you think?" Martin whispered.

"I don't like it," Pedro whispered back.

"Me neither."

"But we have no choice, Martin."

"You're right. Where do you think . . . ?" But as they turned a corner, Martin stopped dead in his tracks. He had never seen anything like it before.

The passage ran in a straight line for as far as he could see. And he *could* see as clearly as though it were daylight. At intervals of twenty yards along the walls, fires burned in small silver cups, fuelled by a hidden oil supply. But it was the walls themselves that caught the light, magnified it and reflected it back. The passage was lined with sheets of solid gold.

Then he saw that they were not intended to make the journey on foot. Six mules and two Indian servants were waiting for them. As he walked towards them, they bowed low and led the mules forward. Martin and Pedro each climbed onto a mule and sat on the brightly covered blankets that were their saddles. Tomac and the others then mounted on their own mules. The sixth was left to carry their supplies and, tied to the reins, Charley.

So began a ride that Martin would never forget. One after another, the flickering oil lamps lit their progress. Nobody spoke. Only the sound of the mules' hooves striking the hard stone floor broke the silence of the corridor. For the first two miles there was nothing to see but their own shimmering reflections in the beaten gold of the walls. Then the passage widened and they passed countless treasures, lined up against the walls: jars and pitchers, cups and trays, idols in the shape of men and women, funeral masks and *tumies*, the ceremonial knives once used by the Incas. Everything was made of gold or silver; some pieces were encrusted with rubies and emeralds, others decorated with fragments of turquoise. The vaults of Fort Knox itself couldn't have contained as much gold as Martin saw that day.

It was only when they halted for a rest that Martin realized how cold he had become. He shivered and, seeing him, Tomac went over to the supply mule. "You were these," he said.

He produced two ponchoes, beautifully woven with gold thread forming patterns against a mauve background. Martin and Pedro slipped their heads through the holes in the centre and let the rich material hang around them.

"Now we must leave the passage," Tomac said. "Climb mountains on Inca Trail."

"What's the Inca Trail?" Martin asked. "And where exactly are we going?"

The Indian smiled for the first time that night. "Inca Trail is path to Machu Picchu," he said. "Now many tourists walk that way. But this way is secret. Only for Inca princes."

After another two miles, they stopped again. The golden panels ended and once again they were plunged into darkness. With his torch, Tomac located a lever set in the wall and pulled it. At once a chink of grey light appeared, growing wider as a huge boulder swung silently open. Leaving the mules with the Indian attendants, they stepped outside. The door closed behind them and when Martin turned to examine it, he found himself looking at the side of a hill covered with shrubs. There wasn't so much as a bent blade of grass to hint at the secrets within.

Eight more Indians were waiting for them on the path, carrying two litters. The moment they saw the boys, they bowed low. Tomac turned to them.

"We carry you," he said. "Kings should not walk."

"Kings?" Martin couldn't help smiling.

"You can carry Charley if you like," Pedro said, "but I think I walk."

"Me too," Martin agreed.

Tomac explained this to the Indians, then returned to the boys. "Very well," he said. "You eat this." He gave them each a handful of leaves wrapped round a small, grey pebble. "The leaves are *coca*," he explained. "The stone we call *llibta*. Chew them well. Help you walk in thin air."

They walked. The path twisted through the jungle, sometimes disappearing into tunnels of trees and flowering shrubs. Sometimes it snaked along in the open, and looking across the valley Martin could see the tiny figures of watchmen, checking their progress from a distance. Now he trod carefully as the path suddenly narrowed with a sheer drop of hundreds of feet only a few inches away. But their Indian guides moved swiftly, ignoring the danger.

Although the coca leaves tasted disgusting, they revived Martin's strength. However, as the sun rose above the mountains and the heat increased, his eyes began to grow heavy. His feet were sore and he was just beginning to wish they hadn't been so hasty about the litters when they arrived at a steep flight of steps cut into the side of the hill.

"Intipunku," Tomac said. "The Sun Gate. We arrive."

Martin shook his head. "Richard is never going to believe a word of this," he said.

They climbed up the staircase and passed through a crumbling gateway. On the other side, on the brow of a hill and surrounded by the ruins of Inca buildings, they saw their destination.

Machu Picchu; the lost city of the Incas. It nestled on a ridge between two craggy mountain peaks, a fantastic fortress of solid stone walls, towers, temples and houses, flanked by terraces like enormous steps on one side and a sheer drop on the other. In the middle of the city, there was what looked like a fireball of light, blazing on a ledge above the main square. Even from a distance, they could see that there were hundreds of people there, lining the passageways and filling the terraces.

"We'd heard that Machu Picchu was closed to tourists," Martin said.

The Indian smiled again. "These are not tourists. My people."

"Who exactly are your people?" Martin asked. But already he had guessed.

"We are the Incas," Tomac said.

Together, the three of them moved forward towards the waiting crowds.

12

Last of the Incas

As Martin and Pedro walked through the ruined city, a hush fell on the Incas. There were more than a thousand of them, all dressed in brightly coloured robes and tunics, some with feathered head-dresses, some wearing heavy gold necklaces and ear-rings. Two rows of soldiers lined the path, carrying spears. The path led to a broad staircase climbing to a long balcony. Tomac paused at the foot of it and the boys turned to him, but the guide shook his head. "I wait here," he said. "Look after the monkey for you. Now you go alone."

Martin climbed to the top of the staircase. Now he saw what he had seen from the brow of the hill, reflecting the sunlight. It was a throne of solid gold, carved with a golden condor on the back and golden snakes along the arms and legs. There were two other thrones, plainer and in silver, one on each side of it. An old man stood behind them, watching him approach.

The man wore a golden crown, decorated with three rows of warriors, also beaten out of gold. Heavy gold beads hung round his neck, saucers of gold dangled from his ears and golden bracelets encircled his arms. He wore a tunic covered with small squares of gold. His skin was wrinkled, burnt a deep brown by the sun.

"Welcome!" he said, raising his arms.

Later on, Martin would be unable to say whether the man spoke in English, Spanish or in some other language. But he and Pedro understood. "Who are you?" he asked.

"I am Roca, Prince of the Sun, emperor of the Incas. Once my fathers ruled over a great empire. Today I have few subjects. These are all that remain." He waved his hand over the crowd. "They have come from all over South America, from the cities where they are forced to work. But they are all true Inca men and women. Their blood is pure."

"What do you want with us?"

"All will be explained." Roca smiled. "Please sit."

Martin moved forward, making for the nearest silver throne. But something inside him stopped him. He paused and glanced at Pedro. Pedro gave him a nod of encouragement. Slowly, deliberately, he lowered himself onto the golden throne. At once a great cry came from the crowd, beginning low and then soaring over the mountains and ringing across the valleys. Pedro sat down beside Martin. From their thrones, the two boys could look over a wide, grassy square separating them from the hosts who now fell silent and sat on the terraces in front of the buildings. Only the Prince of the Sun remained standing. He stepped forward and in a loud, clear voice began to speak.

"Four hundred and fifty years ago," he began, "one of the mightiest empires ever built fell and died. With the coming of the conquistadors from Spain, everything we had lived for was destroyed. Our cities were burned down, our gold looted, our temples desecrated. Our lands were seized, our ancient rights usurped. So began for us the time of the great darkness.

"Today, the glory of the Inca world is no more than a memory. Our cities are ruins, the broken pieces laid bare for tourists. Our art is locked away in museums. And we, the descendants of the Incas, we are forced to conceal our very existence. We have no place in the modern world. Only when we meet in secret can we call ourselves by our true name." He raised his voice, his words resounding around the city. "The last of the Incas."

He fell silent. Martin looked at the listening Indians. Nobody moved. Only a soft wind, rustling in the grass, disturbed the silence.

"But we have not lost our strength." Roco turned to Martin and Pedro. "You have seen only a small part of our secret world, a fraction of the gold that we hid from the Spaniards. We have assembled here today to show ourselves to you. For when your final struggle comes, you must know that you can call on us."

He turned again to the Incas. "A new world is dawning. In that world, we would regain our rightful place. Once again our society would flourish, our laws, our justice, our peace. But we will achieve nothing unless we are prepared to fight for it. And our enemies are more deadly than the conquistadors ever were. The Old Ones. We have always known of them. They seek to destroy the new world before it is even born. And they are here in Peru.

"Before the sun has risen and set three times, the Old Ones will break through the gate that was created in Peru when the world began. One boy will stand against them and alone he will fall. This the *amautas*, our wise men, have seen. They have read the signs in the sky and on the land. The rain falls where there should be no rain. There are too many stars in the heavens at night. A terrible disaster is but a heartbeat away and perhaps all our hopes will come to nothing. One boy will stand against the Old Ones and alone he will fall. The *amautas* have spoken."

A low murmuring rippled across the assembled Incas.

Martin and Pedro glanced at one another. "One boy alone," the Inca had said. But which one?

"But not all is lost," Roca continued. "Five defeated them at the dawn of time and five shall rise up against them again. So runs the ancient prophecy. Martin Hopkins is the first of the five. His powers have led him to the second, the boy who is also our king. Three others must still be found. For only when the five have come together will they have the power to defeat the Old Ones. Only then can the last great war take place and the new world begin.

"So let us celebrate today. Though dark things are still to come, today our king is with us. The first of the five brought him to us. No matter what happens, today the Inca Empire lives again."

At once the music struck up again. Tables and chairs were brought out into the green square and canopies erected to keep them in the shade. Huge fires were lit under cauldrons and plates of meat and vegetables were carried forward. Soon the air was filled with the smell of bubbling stews and the laughter and feasting began.

Whether it was the maize wine he was drinking or the sheer exuberance of the Incas, for Martin the afternoon seemed to rush forward like a big dipper at a fun-fair. He heard songs about the exploits of Inca warriors. He ate tropical fruit and cakes. The wine never stopped flowing. Slowly the sun moved behind the emerald peak that overlooked the city, its golden glow tinged with the deep red of the coming evening.

Martin and Pedro had become separated during the banquet, although Martin had spotted Charley, stuffed with food, sound asleep on one of the litters. As the cool of the night set in, he left the table and went in search of his friend. At last he saw him. Pedro was sitting, slightly to one side, deep in conversation with Roca. As he approached, the two of them looked up and called out for him to join them.

"Pedro has been telling me of your adventures," Roca said as Martin sat down.

"Maybe you can help us," Martin said. "I have the page . . ."

But before he could produce the page from the diary, Roca stopped him. "This is not the time or place," he said. "And I am not the right person. The archaeologist, Professor Chambers, is the one you must speak with. Chambers has the answers that you need. Already I have sent messengers. The professor will be in Cuzco tomorrow. There you will meet."

"May I ask you a question?" Pedro said.

"Of course."

Pedro paused. "All that stuff about the five, about fighting the Old Ones . . . I understand that, sort of. And, I mean, I know Martin is pretty special. But you called me your king. Now, I didn't know anything about the Incas until today. So how can I be your king?"

"I will answer your question," Roca said. "But I warn you, Pedro. The answer may not leave you any the wiser.

"Let me tell you, first, how the Inca world began. According to our stories, in the beginning—thousands of years ago—there was only darkness. The land was bare and the people lived like animals. Then the father of all things whom we call Vicarocha—the Sun—decided to send his son down to teach the people how to live properly, how to cultivate the fields and build houses.

"And so came Manco Capac into the world, rising out of the waters of Lake Titicaca, son of the Sun, first of the Incas. Manco travelled the world until at last he came to a valley near Cuzco. Here he plunged a gold rod into the earth for this was the place where he would found the Inca empire.

"For many years he ruled wisely and strongly before returning to the heavens. In that time, one image was made of him. It was engraved on a great disc of gold. This treasure, more precious to us than any other, was called the Sun of Viracocha. When the conquistadors came, it was hidden away and nobody has seen it since though many have tried to find it."

He raised an arm. On the far side of the square, two lines of soldiers moved forward carrying flaming beacons. Then eight more Incas appeared, bowing under the weight of a huge litter. Something flat and circular rested on top, covered by a cloth. All round the city, heads turned silently to follow the treasure. The carriers set it down a few yards in front of Pedro. Then, with a gesture from Roca, the cloth was removed.

For a moment the golden disc dazzled Pedro and he was able to see. It seemed to shine with a light of its own. The disc had been fashioned like a sun, with golden flames writhing round its rim. He blinked and screwed up his eyes. Gradually he was able to make out a face, engraved on the surface. It was a face that he recognized, but still it took him another minute to realize.

"There is your answer," the Prince of the Sun said.

"No . . ." Pedro began. But there could be no doubt. He was looking at a portrait of himself.

13

Professor Chambers

The next morning, Roca walked down with Martin, Pedro and Charley to the railway station that had been built at the foot of Machu Picchu. "The tourist train is running again," he said. "It will take you back to Cuzco."

"I wish we didn't have to go alone," Martin said.

"There is no danger. Messengers have told me that the German has flown back to Lima. And there is nothing to be gained by our going with you." He handed Martin a slip of paper. "If you have any further need of us, use this as a means of contacting us."

Martin looked at the paper. "A telephone number!" he exclaimed.

Roca smiled. "Even the Incas cannot ignore progress. Call the number and a message will reach me. Do not hesitate to use it if the need is there."

The Inca waited with them on the deserted station platform until they heard the sound of a train approaching. "I must leave you now," Roca said. "But we will meet again."

The train pulled into the station and Martin and Pedro climbed onto it. They turned round to say goodbye. But Roca had already disappeared.

Martin and Pedro were virtually alone on the train back to Cuzco. They sat facing each other. Charley curled up on the table between them and dozed.

"What happens in Cuzco?" Pedro asked.

"Chambers," Martin said. "Tomac gave me the name of a hotel; the Familiar. Chambers should be there."

The boys were too tired to talk any more. Soon Pedro fell asleep, the face on the disc shimmering in his dreams. Martin stayed awake longer. The words of the Inca still rang in his ears. "One will stand against them . . . he alone will fall." He could hear Roca's voice, echoing in the rhythm of the wheels. "Fall . . . he will fall . . . he will fall . . ." Slowly the train wove its way through the grey-lit mountains. There were just three days left.

The man from the embassy threw a packet of cigarettes onto the table. "They're not good for you," he remarked.

Richard grabbed them gratefully. "Peru isn't good for me." He lit one and sat back in his chair. "So what's the news?"

"Bad I'm afraid," Mr. Knights said. "The embassy can't help you."

"But I told you everything."

"That's right. It's a terrific story. Petrol tankers with a mind of their own. Boys with magic powers. German assassins, devils, mad monks and God knows what else." Mr. Knights shook his head. "If the British ambassador tried to get you released with a story like that, he'd probably find himself locked up with you. In a lunatic asylum."

Richard had been in prison for almost a week now. During that time he had lost half a stone in weight and he had become so dishevelled that he looked more like a scarecrow than a journalist. His eyes were red from lack of sleep. He hadn't found it easy to drop off knowing that there was a mass-murderer in the bunk above him.

"If only we had something more . . . believable to go on," Mr. Knights continued. "For example, if you could tell me what the Hopkins boy was up to in Tovar's office . . ."

"I've already said!" Richard interrupted. "TC Lima, that's the link. Tovar must be the man behind it all."

"But that's ridiculous," the embassy official said. "Victor Valenzuela de Tovar is one of the most respected men in the country. His company has done more to modernize Peru than any other. Why, only yesterday he launched a brand new satellite into orbit, paid for out of his own pocket. If it weren't for Tovar, there probably wouldn't even be telephones in Peru, let alone space rockets and all the rest of it. I tell you, Mr. Cole, the man is the nearest thing they've got to a saint."

The two men paused. Then Richard leant forward, pointing with his cigarette. "Listen to me, Mr. Knights," he said. "You asked me for the truth and I told you. Any day now the Old Ones are going to break into Peru and that will be the end of it. Martin is out there by himself and he needs my help. You've got to get me released from here. I don't care how you do it."

"I can't do it," Mr. Knights cried. "Don't you understand? Unless you can come up with a more believable story, you're stuck here. For twenty years, Mr. Cole. That's the sentence for drug smuggling. And there's nothing we can do to help."

Rochard closed his eyes. "Then it's all up to Martin," he said. "He's on his own. And if he fails, then we all lose."

The Hostal Familiar was situated about ten minutes from the Plaza de Armas. It was a clean and attractive building with two floors surrounding a flower-filled courtyard. A door beside the main entrance led into a small coffee room which also acted as a reception area.

It was ten o'clock in the morning when Martin and Pedro walked in, another hot Cuzco day.

The coffee bar was empty but for two people. One, a Peruvian, was standing behind the counter, leaning over a selection of home-made cakes. The other was an Englishwoman—and anyone more out-of-place in the Inca capital would be hard to imagine.

Despite the weather, she was dressed in an old-fashioned tweed suit with an off-white shirt buttoned up to the neck. She was an immensely large woman with thick legs and a torso that seemed to continue down to her thighs without any obvious sign of a waist. Her hair, done up in a bun, was somewhere between brown and grey with most of the colour drawn out by the sun. Her face, untouched by any make-up, was tanned and windbeaten. She must have been in her fifties, Martin thought, although her voice was that of a younger woman.

She was talking in fast but accented Spanish, accompanying her words with violent movements of her hands. Martin waited for her to stop talking but as she gave no sign of ever doing so, he eventually interrupted.

"Excuse me . . ." he said, addressing the man.

The woman turned and glared at him. "I'm talking," she announced, quite unnecessarily for her voice could have been heard all over Cuzco.

"I'm sorry," Martin said, "but it's important." He turned to the man again. "Do you have a Professor Chambers staying here?" he asked.

The woman coughed loudly. "I am Professor Chambers," she announced.

Martin stared at her, his mouth falling open.

"Don't gape, boy!" she said. "What's the matter with you?"

"Well . . ." Martin was lost for words.

Pedro stepped forward. "We were expecting . . ."

"A man!" The professor sniffed. "Typical! Well, I am Professor Chambers and if you want to speak to me, you'd better get on with it. I have just come back from an extremely important excavation and I don't intend to hang around. Who are you, anyway?"

"I'm Pedro."

"And I'm Martin."

"Delighted to meet you."

The Professor rapped out an order to the man behind the counter who immediately began to prepare cakes and coffee for three. Then she sat down at one of the tables and told the boys to join her. At that moment, Charley sprang into life. He had been crouching on Pedro's shoulder, hidden by his head. But seeing Chambers, he leapt off and before anyone could stop him, reached out and pulled the Professor's nose.

"Desist!" Chambers cried. Pedro bounded forward and dragged Charley away. "What a despicable creature!" the Professor exclaimed. "How impossibly nasty! Remove it at once!"

Pedro tied Charley to an adjoining table while Martin tried to apologize. Fortunately the coffee and three huge slices of chocolate cake arrived and the Professor regained her composure. As they were soon to discover, she had a gargantuan appetite.

"As I was trying to tell you, before that malevolent mammal assaulted me," she began, plunging her fork into the cake, "I was called back last night from an important archaeological excavation outside Cuzco. According to the radio message, there was a matter of extreme urgency needing my attention here in Cuzco."

"That's true," Pedro said.

"You sent the message?"

"No," Martin told her. "It was a friend of ours."

"And what could two somewhat tatty adolescents want that could possibly concern me?"

"It's a long story," Pedro said.

"Very well. In that case . . . more cake!"

Once again, Martin told his story. This time, however, he left out the more fantastic elements, convinced that the Professor would never believe him. He began with the auction and the murder of the antique dealer. Then he described his arrival in Lima, Richard's arrest and his meeting with Pedro. He told her about their adventures in Tovar's office and his discovery of the page from the diary. But any mention of the Incas and his own powers he left out.

Professor Chambers listened to him in silence apart from the occasional "Humph!" or "Hah!" But watching her closely, Martin was sure that she believed him. She seemed to know of the Old Ones and even as she attacked her cake, he could see that she was deep in thought. At last he finished. For a minute, nobody spoke.

"That is quite a story, young man," Chambers said at last.

"It's all true!" Pedro protested.

"It may be true. But it's not all. You haven't told me everything, have you?"

"No," Martin admitted.

"Well, we shall ignore that for the moment. The page from the diary . . . do you have it with you?"

"It's here." Martin produced it from his pocket.

Professor Chambers unfolded it and examined it closely. "Yes . . ." she muttered. "Yes . . . as I thought." She slammed the paper down on the table. "We must leave for Nazca."

"Nazca?" Pedro said.

"When?" Martin asked.

"Immediately. I have a private plane at Cuzco airport. And although I'm but a mere slip of a woman . . ." she glanced at Pedro, ". . . I am also a qualified pilot. We must leave this minute." She waved a finger at the two boys. "But I warn you, both of you, if you allow your preposterous pet to come anywhere near me—I shall eject it!"

The plane was a five-seater Cessna. There could have been a long delay at Cuzco airport as the control tower wouldn't give them clearance to take off. However Professor Chambers ignored the commands coming over the radio, manoeuvred the plane onto the main runway and with the crackle of official complaint in her ears, accelerated and took off.

The flight took three hours. With the noise of the engine, it was difficult to talk and Martin and Pedro were content to relax. As they left the Andes behind them and approached their destination, however, the Professor turned round. "Look out of the window," she shouted.

All Martin could see was desert. "What is it?" he asked.

Professor Chambers pulled back on the joy-stick and the plane dipped down. "The Nazca Lines," she said. "They're the reason why you came to Peru."

Martin gazed out of the window, but still he could see nothing. Then he caught his breath. There was a line, drawn in the sand, running dead straight for as far as his eye could see. The plane turned in a tight arc and now he saw a huge shape. It was a rectangle, narrower at one end than at the other. It must have been at least a mile long. Staring out of the other window, Pedro reached back and nudged him. There were more lines, running in all directions, crossing over one another, all as straight as arrows. Martin looked in wonderment. The whole desert was nothing less than a fantastic doodling pad on a gigantic scale.

But there were greater wonders to come. As the plane tilted and curved, Martin saw what looked like a picture. At first he thought he was imagining things, but it was there. It was a bird, its outstretched wings running for hundreds of feet. More straight lines ran over it, as if someone had tried to cross it out, but the shape was unmistakeable.

One by one, a fantastic menagerie of animals appeared on the surface of the desert, each animal perfectly drawn. There was a monkey with a spiralling tail, a whale, a condor and a huge spider. Some of the shapes were less recognizable. They flew over what looked like a blob with one outstretched hand; it lay beside a modern road that ran right through the desert. How had the pictures come to be there, Martin wondered? What fantastic imagination had conceived them? And why?

Professor Chambers turned the plane round and twenty minutes later they touched down at Nazca airport—no more than a strip of rubble and two sheds. The Professor docked the plane and switched off the engine.

"Well?" she demanded.

"I . . . I don't understand," Martin said.

"It's simple," Chambers said. "You told me you came to Peru looking for a gate. And now you have seen the Nazca Lines. If your gate really exists, and if it is about to be opened, then that is where it's to be found."

14

The Nazca Lines

Professor Chambers lived in one of the most beautiful houses Martin and Pedro had ever seen. It was situated in a garden the size of a park just outside the town of Nazca. Flowers blossomed in urns and exotic trees cast cool shadows over the lawns. A llama and two goats wondered freely about and dozens of birds, brilliant in the afternoon sunlight, filled the air with colour and song. Two houses stood in the grounds. The Professor lived in a low, white building with a sweeping, green-tiled roof and a broad verandah shaded by a colonnade. The second building, similar but smaller and separated by a stream, was reserved for guests. A crumbling white wall, with a gate at the bottom of a winding driveway, completely encircled the garden.

"How can you make the money for a place like this?" Pedro asked. "Maybe that's a rude question," he added quickly.

"It certainly is a rude question," Chambers snapped. "But the answer is, the Peruvian government pays for it." She sniffed. "It is in recognition of my services to archaeology and in particular to the Nazca Lines."

"The Nazca Lines . . ." Martin repeated.

"Exactly. I think it is time you were educated. Quite frankly, I'm amazed that you have never heard of them. They are, after all, one of the wonders of the ancient world."

The three of them were sitting on the verandah overlooking the garden. Charley, on the Professor's orders, had been locked in a room inside the house. Now Chambers dug into a bulging case and pulled out a sheet of paper. "This is cut out of a magazine," she explained. "It will, I suppose, serve as a general introduction to the lines. Read and absorb!"

Martin took the article and laid it on the table between Pedro and himself. They began to read:

THE MYSTERY OF THE NAZCA LINES

Stonehenge, the Pyramids, Loch Ness . . . even in the twentieth century, the world is full of mysteries: man-made and natural phenomena that science cannot explain. Among these mysteries, none is more striking nor more peculiar than the Nazca Lines.

The Nazca desert is a vast wasteland, a barren plateau on a grand scale. It was here that, around 600 AD, the ancient Indians of Nazca drew a series of extraordinary designs in the ground. Most beautiful of these are the animals: a whale, a condor, a monkey, a humming bird (with a wing-span of over 200 feet) and a huge spider. In addition, there are triangles, spirals and star shapes as well as thousands of perfectly straight lines, some of them stretching for up to twenty-five miles.

The mystery begins when you understand that the Nazca Lines are so big that you <u>can only see them from the air.</u> In fact the lines were only discovered in 1927 when one of the first aeroplanes in Peru flew over them. Obviously the Nazcan people didn't have any aeroplanes in 600 AD. So why did they go to the *trouble of scratching out the lines and the pictures when they could never see them?*

All sorts of theories have been put forward. Were the lines an airport for spaceships from another planet? Were they drawn for the benefit of the ancient gods in the sky? Some suggest that they had a religious meaning, while many experts believe that they were in some way tied to the stars, perhaps being used to forecast the seasons. But nobody knows for certain.

Today, visitors often fly over the lines, simply marvelling at their size and beauty. Meanwhile, the scientists, archaeologists and astronomers are spending hours, weeks or even months trying to unlock their secret. One woman, the English archaeologist, Augusta Chambers, has spent no less than seventeen years studying them. But apart from her belief that the lines are some sort of prophetic warning, she has still failed to publish any definite answers.

We are fortunate that, due to the uniquely dry weather conditions in Nazca, the lines exist to this day. But we're still not certain when they were drawn. We have only a rough idea of how they were drawn. And exactly why they were drawn remains the greatest mystery of all.

"Do you begin to see?" Chambers asked when they had finished.

"The lines on the page from the diary . . ." Martin began.

"Well done!" She produced the photo-copy and set it down beside the article. "These lines are a detail of part of the Nazca Lines."

"But which part?" Pedro asked.

"That's simple. The poem gives you the answer. The place of Qolqa . . . you saw it from the plane. Qolqa is a word in the ancient language of Peru. It means 'granary'. And it's the name given to the great rectangle we flew over."

"Stand before the place of Qolqa . . ." Martin read. His eyes lit up. "That means the gate must be in front of the rectangle!"

The Professor shook her head. "There is no gate in the desert," she said. "There are no standing stones. No buildings. There's just the sand and the lines."

"What does the scorpion mean?" Pedro asked, pointing to the first line of the poem.

"Tovar—he said something about a scorpion."

"That's another mystery. The lines depict all sorts of animals, but there are no scorpions."

"Are you sure?" Martin asked.

"Young man!" the Professor flared. "The day I started studying the Nazca Lines, you weren't even born. Of course I'm sure!"

She produced a sandwich from her briefcase and devoured it in three mouthfuls.

"Listen," she continued when she had finished. "I am *the* expert on the Nazca Lines. I have published four books on the subject. And more to the point, I have spent the last ten years protecting the wretched things.

"You must understand that the lines only survived because nobody knew they were there—or at least, that's what I always thought. Clearly your mad monk somehow managed to stumble onto them. Anyway, all that changed once they'd been seen from the air. These days, thousands of tourists come to Nazca to see them. And if they had their way, they'd trample all over them too—never mind the fact that their footprints would destroy them in a matter of days.

"But the reason why I moved to Nazca, and the reason why the government pays me to stay here, is that I have protected the lines. I have guards watching over them. It is forbidden to walk in the desert without special permission and I alone have that permission."

"In the office . . ." Pedro said, "they were afraid you'd turn up."

"Of course." Chambers nodded. "Tovar wanted to take a close look at the lines so he had to wait until I was out of the way. Once I was gone, my guards wouldn't have been so worried about taking a bribe."

"But if there isn't a gate in the desert," Martin said, "what did Tovar hope to find?"

"I don't know," Chambers admitted. She looked at her watch. "But the sooner we find out, the better. We have only three days . . ."

"How do *you* know it's only three days?"

"It's on the page you found, Martin. Inti Raymi."

"What's Inti Raymi?"

"It's a major festival in Peru, the time of the summer solstice when the sun is at its farthest point south of the Equator. June 24th. And today is June 21st. Three days. I don't know for sure what we'll find at the place of Qolqa. But the sooner we get there the better."

"Martin Hopkins," Mr. Todd whispered. Never had two words been uttered with more venom. "That boy bears a charmed life. I could have broken his neck in London. And in Cuzco . . ."

"In Cuzco you lost him." Victor Valenzuela de Tovar finished the sentence coldly. "Two boys loose in a small town. A simple job. And you bungled it."

"Next time . . ."

"There will be no next time!"

The industrialist smiled, two dark spots appearing in his cheeks. "There is nothing Hopkins can do," he said. "My figures have been checked and double checked and the golden scorpion is fully operational." He laughed briefly. "Forget about the boy, Mr. Todd."

"What if he finds Chambers? What if they go into the desert?"

"Then they will die." The industrialist lowered his voice, although there was nobody else in the room to hear. "The Old Ones have other servants," he said, "and not all of them are human ones. I hope the boy does go to the Place of Qolqa. For there he will be on the threshhold of the gate. There he will be close to the Old Ones. And there they will destroy him, for once and for all."

15

On the Threshold

Martin could see nothing of the lines nor even the great rectangle which he knew must begin only a few yards in front of him. At ground level, he could see no more than a flat, empty plateau—a *pampa*, Professor Chambers had called it. There was nothing for miles in any direction. Only where the desert was bordered by two mountain ranges with a brief gap in the middle could any upright shapes be seen. And even these were disappearing in the rapidly fading light.

But there could be no doubt that someone had been here before them. The desert was like the surface of the moon. Any mark made there stayed. The track marks of a car and dozens of fresh footprints had made an easy path to follow. And although the visitors had done the best to conceal their handiwork, a wide area showed up white against the grey-yellow desert where the sand had recently been dug up.

Now Martin and Pedro were hard at work with spades, re-exposing whatever it was that Tovar's men had found at the place of Qolqa. Although the sun was setting, it was still terribly hot. The dust had clogged their throats, stung their eyes and settled in their hair.

Their sweat made muddy tracks as it trickled down their faces. But the sand, already disturbed once, came away easily. In only an hour they had dug a trench almost three feet deep. Meanwhile, Professor Chambers had erected two tents and built a fire with wood brought from Nazca. If necessary, they would stay the night and begin again the next morning.

"No slacking!" the Professor called out as she tied the last ropes on the second tent.

With a groan, Martin thrust his spade into the sand. There was a clang. Pedro, working a few paces away, looked up.

Hastily, the two boys began to scoop away. Slowly, something flat and square appeared. It was a brick platform, decorated by some sort of design in the centre. As they cleared the sand away, more of the design was revealed. At last they could see it.

Professor Chambers hurried over to the two boys and looked down into the pit. "I take it that this is the sign you described," she said. "The sign of the Old Ones."

"Yes," Martin whispered. He shivered. The desert seemed cold. "This is the sign."

"But what is this thing it's on?" Pedro asked.

"It's a platform." The Professor peered more closely at it. "About ten feet square, I would say. The bricks are made of andesite. Nothing odd about that. But the design—that's quite wrong."

"Do you understand what it's doing here?" Martin asked.

"Not completely. But I have a good idea." Now it was the Professor's turn to shiver.

"Let's get the fire lit," she suggested. "We'd better talk."

Ten minutes later, the three of them were sitting cross-legged round a roaring fire, drinking tea. Apart from the crackle of the flames, all was silent in the great emptiness of the desert.

"I'll try to keep this simple," the Professor said, "although it's actually jolly complicated. I have described to you the mystery of the Nazca Lines. Now I must tell you one solution to the mystery. It was the subject of a book I wrote many years ago." She fell silent for a moment. "Perhaps Tovar read my book," she continued at length. "Perhaps, in a way, I'm to blame for what's happening. Still, listen carefully, and I'll try to explain . . .

"I've studied the lines, as I told you, for more than seventeen years. At first, it was just an interest for me. But as time passed, I came to believe that they . . . that there was something evil about them. The pictures of the animals are beautiful—I don't deny it. But it crossed my mind that to the ancient Nazca people, to whoever drew them, they must have been terrifying too. Huge spiders. Monstrous whales. Unearthly blobs. Even the monkey is grotesque, reaching out with its spindly arms. And it's deformed. It has only four fingers on one hand. Why do you think the people who drew the lines gave it one finger too few?"

"Maybe they couldn't count," Pedro suggested.

"Maybe. But in primitive societies, deformity is often something to be feared, a bad omen. Maybe that's the point. All the animals could have been drawn simply to scare people."

"You're scaring me," Pedro muttered.

"Now, all the experts are agreed that the Nazca Lines are connected with the stars," the Professor continued. "I myself studied astronomy and when I first saw the Nazca Lines, I thought they might be some sort of huge star map.

"I believed that the lines had been drawn to point at stars at certain times of the year. You'd stand on a line and look down it and if you saw a star rising above the horizon at the other end, then you'd know it was April 5th and time to start planting the grain or whatever. But as I continued my studies, I became obsessed by the idea that perhaps there might be a moment, no less than a few minutes in a thousand years, when *all* the lines would point to *all* the visible stars at the same time. Now that would be . . . Am I boring you, young man?"

Martin was sitting on the other side of the fire, his head turned upwards, gazing at the night sky. He had been listening to begin with, but something had distracted him. What was it? There were no sounds in the desert. Could he have imagined it? No. There it was again, a soft beating in the air, like a tent flap in the wind. Only there was no wind. He waited, his ears pricked. But it had gone.

"Are you listening?" the Professor asked.

With an effort, Martin turned to face her. "Yes," he stammered. "Of course."

"Good. This is where things get complicated.

"As I was saying, I wanted all the stars to line up with all the Nazca Lines. How would they do this? Well, imagine that you could lie on your back on the desert floor and take a photograph of the night sky. You'd end up with a big sheet of paper with lots of little dots on it. The little dots would be stars. Then you could go up in the air and take a photograph of the lines, making a second picture. Well, what I was looking for was a time when the stars in the first picture would fall exactly on the lines in the second picture . . ."

"A sort of join-the-dots on a big scale," Martin said.

"That's more or less it.

"Anyway, this won't happen very often. I would have liked to have checked it out, but of course it wasn't possible."

"Why not?" Pedro asked.

"Because I didn't know the spot where you'd have to stand to see the stars in their correct position. I needed to find an observation platform." She gestured towards the trench. "A platform like that.

"You see, the stars always seem to be moving when you look at them from the Earth. The reason for this is, of course, that it's the Earth that's moving—spinning on its own axis. That's why the stars never seem to be in the same position.

"And it gets even more tricky when you remember that the earth isn't only spinning. It's also orbiting around the sun. And as it orbits, it wobbles. Astronomers call this wobble precession. And what precession means is that the earth is only in exactly the same position once every twenty-six thousand years.

"So to go right back to where I started, what I wondered and what I wrote about in my book, was suppose that the Nazca Lines were drawn as a sort of terrible warning? Suppose that what they were doing was recording a moment in time, one moment in twenty-six thousand years, when they would finally line up with the stars? That would explain why the pictures were so frightening. It would explain why they had to be drawn in the first place."

"And you think the lines will line up in two nights from now?" Martin asked.

"Now that I've found the platform, I can check it. But . . ."

The Professor broke off again. This time it was Pedro whose attention seemed to have wandered. "Pedro?" she snapped.

"I'm sorry . . ." Pedro narrowed his eyes. "There's something . . ."

"What?"

"I heard it too," Martin said.

The fire was still burning, throwing deep red shadows over the sand. The Landrover stood where it had been parked. The night had grown cool and now there was a faint touch of a breeze in the air. Pedro looked up at the sky, at the millions of glistening stars. For a moment he thought he saw two tiny green lights. He shook his head. There was no such thing as a green star . . .

"You're imagining things," the Professor said. "The desert does that to you sometimes. There's nothing out here."

"The platform . . ." Martin began.

"The platform marks the exact position where you have to stand to see the stars," the Professor continued. That's what it said in the verse you showed me. Stand before the place of Qolqa and you will see the light . . ."

". . . that is the end of all light," Martin finished the sentence.

The Professor nodded gravely. "There you have it again. The warning. This is the place. And if our friend the monk got his sums right, the time is just two days from now."

"That's when the gate will open," Martin said.

The Professor shook her head. "But there is no gate in the desert, Martin. I've told you . . ."

Pedro was the first to see them. The two green lights were back, burning in the air, high above them but moving downwards. Even as the Professor spoke he made out a dark shape behind the lights. It seemed to be coming right at them.

There was a ghastly shriek. Martin dived flat onto the sand as an enormous bird plummeted towards him, steel-like claws reaching out for his eyes. He felt a seering pain in his shoulder, heard the cloth of his shirt tear as the bird ripped through. Then it had wheeled away and all was silent once again but for the beating of its huge wings in the night air.

Martin rolled over and got dizzily to his feet.

"What was it?" Pedro demanded.

"A condor," the Professor said. "But it's impossible . . ."

Martin pointed upwards. "It's coming back," he cried.

There was a sudden thudding in the air. The three of

them fell back as the monstrous bird rushed past, its green eyes blazing. The bird was huge, its feathers hanging off its body like a ragged cloak. Its beak curved out of its bald head like a dagger. Its talons were open, the points as sharp as razors. For a moment it was between them, suspended over the fire, then it swooped upwards, disappearing into the night.

Martin leapt up. Running forward, he snatched a burning piece of wood from the fire.

"Get into the Landrover!" he shouted at the Professor. "Hurry!"

"The keys . . . They're in my tent," the Professor cried.

"I'll get them!" Pedro sprang forward, ducking low as a second bird soared down, its outstretched wings buffeting the air only inches from his head.

Within seconds there were six of them hovering over the camp and even as Pedro and Martin began to move, more joined the deadly circle, their dreadful eyes shining in the darkness. Pedro dived into the Professor's tent, searching for the keys to the Landrover. Meanwhile, Chambers had struggled onto the car and was pulling at a bundle on the roof.

Still the condors hung back. Now there were more than a dozen of them, a dense cloud of black shapes, wheeling closer and closer to the camp. It seemed as if they were afraid, but as each second passed and more of them appeared, they grew more confident. Pedro sprinted back to the fire and seized another flaming branch.

"Where are the keys?" Martin shouted.

"It's too dark. I can't find them."

With an ear-splitting shriek, the largest of the condors plummeted downwards, hurtling towards Martin, its claws reaching out.

Martin swung the branch. It hit the bird in the middle of the neck, the flames erupting over its body. With a terrible screech, it somersaulted backwards, crashing to the ground. But a second bird had followed it. Pedro lunged out with his fire-brand but somehow it managed to twist away and then it had fixed itself onto his back, its claws acting like grappling irons, its beak stabbing at his neck. With a cry, he dropped the branch and fell back on the sand, his hands groping for the bird's throat. Martin ran forward. Using his branch like a club, he brought it whistling down. The condor screamed and relaxed its hold. Martin swung again. There was a sickening crunch as wood smashed into bone and feather. The condor curled up in an ugly ball and lay still.

Martin began to realize that they were hopelessly outnumbered. Three more condors were sweeping down, their eyes ablaze. His only weapon had broken in half. He was unarmed. Pedro was still lying at his feet, dazed. Then there was an explosion, followed by two more in quick succession. Professor Chambers was standing on the roof of the Landrover, holding a rifle. Two of the birds crashed into the sand. The third weaved crazily away, one wing shattered.

Martin examined Pedro by the light of the fire. His shirt was torn to ribbons and there was blood oozing from six parallel scratches across his shoulders. "I've got to get the keys," he said. "We'll be safe in the car."

"It's too dark, Martin. You'll never find them."

"It's our only chance."

There was a fourth explosion and another condor spiralled out of the sky. Martin glanced at the Landrover as he ran from the tent. "Look out!" he shouted. Professor Chambers turned round in time to see a pair of brilliant green eyes rushing towards her. With both hands, she rammed the rifle backwards, clubbing the butt into the condor's head. The blow saved her, but now another bird had swooped out of nowhere, throwing her off balance. With a cry, she dropped the gun and fell to her knees, beating with her hands at the condor, trying to keep its claws from her eyes.

Ignoring his own injury, Pedro got up and sprinted

towards her. He reached the Landrover and pulled himself onto the roof. The Professor was lying on her back, the condor on top of her. Pedro threw himself forward. Somehow his hands reached past the great wings and fastened on its throat. He twisted with all his strength. There was a dry crack and the bird fell limp. He knelt beside the Professor.

Meanwhile, Martin had reached the tent, but just outside the flap, he suddenly stopped. For a long moment he stood there, his legs apart, his arms hanging at his sides.

Pedro gazed upwards. To his horror, he saw that the fantastic creatures had more than trebled their number. Now there were more than fifty of them, a whirling, pounding mass that seemed to grow with every passing second. He looked down and saw Martin. It seemed that his friend had given up—but what more was there that they could do? The fire had burnt low. They had lost the gun. They could only wait for what he knew would be the final onslaught.

As one, the throng of condors screamed, the ghastly sound echoing across the desert.

Martin raised his hands. "Pedro!" he cried. "Now! You must help me now!"

Pedro would never be able to describe the feeling. One moment he was looking up, wondering what Martin meant. The next he was shuddering as something like a wave of electricity rushed through him. Then it was as if he was no longer on the roof of the car but standing next to Martin. It seemed almost as if he was Martin. The two had become one.

Professor Chambers stared in disbelief. She stared as the power of the sun flowed through Martin. Vivid beams of white light seemed to burst out of his outstretched palms. They shot through the night like incredible lasers, searing through the darkness. For a moment he stood like a statue, the brilliant beams pouring out of him. Then the light hit the dense cloud of condors. At once they exploded, a huge ball of blinding flame that illuminated the desert for a mile around.

And abruptly it was over. The light disappeared and Martin's arms fell to his side. On the roof of the Landrover, Pedro let out a deep sigh. A few glowing cinders, all that was left of the condors, drifted down to the ground. The darkness, punctured only by the stars, settled on the desert.

Professor Chambers and Pedro climbed down and rejoined Martin beside the tent. "I don't believe it," Chambers muttered. "I don't believe it."

Pedro gazed at Martin, his eyes wide. "That was great, Martin! How did you do it?"

Martin looked back at his friend. He smiled weakly. "I didn't do it," he said. "We did."

16

Artificial Star

"I'm wrong," Professor Chambers said. "I don't understand it. But I've checked and double checked."

"What do you mean?" Martin asked.

"The stars! That's what I mean." The Professor dropped a sheaf of computer print-outs onto the table and sat down. "I was certain that tomorrow night the stars would line up perfectly with the Nazca Lines—just as I described to you. But they don't. It's close. I doubt if it will ever get closer. But one star will be missing, hidden behind the moon."

"Which star?"

"Antares. It's a red giant—far, far bigger than the sun. If you were standing on the platform at the Place of Qolqa at exactly midnight tomorrow, you'd look for it between the two mountain ranges. All the other stars would be in the right place. But Antares wouldn't be anywhere to be seen. It would be about thirty degrees off course, hidden behind the moon."

"Maybe you made a mistake," Pedro suggested.

"Young man! I never make mistakes!"

It was one o'clock on the following afternoon and the three of them were on the verandah at the Professor's house. A meal had been prepared for them, but none of them were eating. Only Charley, reunited with Pedro, helped himself to tomatoes and lettuce leaves, occasionally trying to tempt the Professor by poking them in her ear.

The two boys were sitting uncomfortably in their chairs, pads of lint dressing bulging under their clothes. Chambers' hands were also covered in plasters and she had had to walk to the table with the help of a stick. None of them had escaped unscathed from the attack.

Martin and Pedro had been alone for much of the day while the Professor had worked out star movements on a microcomputer in her house, basing her calculations on the position of the platform. They had been sure that the results would support her theory about the lines. Instead it seemed that they were back to square one.

"If only Richard were here," Martin muttered.

"I doubt if he would be able to make much sense of it either," the Professor said.

"It's not that. In fact Richard would be more muddled than the rest of us. It's just that I miss him. I mean, he's been locked up for ages now. It must be pretty awful for him."

Chambers softened. "I'll make some telephone calls this afternoon," she said. "I have some friends in Lima and they may be able to do something. I wouldn't worry about him, Martin. He's probably better off right now where he is."

Pedro leant forward. "Look," he said. "You say the stars aren't going to do this lining after all. So tell me. What's Tovar going to do?"

"I wish I knew," Chambers muttered. She reached out to pluck a radish from the bowl. "All I know is that my sums can't be wrong. However you look at it, there's one star too few."

"One star too many," Martin mused. "That's what the Incas said. Too many stars, not too few."

"The Incas?" the Professor repeated.

Martin paused. "I'd better tell you," he said. "Although I doubt if you'll believe it."

"After the last forty-eight hours with you two," Chambers said, "I think I'd believe anything."

So Martin told her of their adventures in Cuzco and Machu Picchu, leaving out only the treasures they had seen and the face on the shield. There was a long silence when he had finished. The Professor shook her head.

"So the Incas did survive," she said. "I often suspected it. But what did they mean? Too many stars. Too few stars. It just doesn't make sense."

She folded her hands underneath her chin. "The monk predicted that tomorrow night, Inti Raymi, would be a night of disaster. That much we know. He had somehow discovered the secret of the lines and the secret drove him mad. Now, Tovar stole the diary because he wanted to know the secret. But if the monk got it wrong, if the stars aren't going to line up . . ."

"Then perhaps it's all been for nothing," Martin suggested. "Perhaps we can all go home."

Chambers sighed. "I wish it were true," she said. "But I don't believe it."

"I don't believe it either," Pedro said.

"There must be something else. Think back . . . What was it that Tovar said when you overheard him in the office?"

Pedro thought hard. It all seemed so long ago. Tovar had been talking about the search for the platform. He had mentioned Chambers. But there had been something else. What was it? His eyes lit up. "I remember something," he said.

"What?"

"It was something about a scorpion. They had to move a golden scorpion. And they said it had to be precise. I didn't understand at the time. I don't get it now."

"There was a scorpion on the front cover of the diary," Martin added. "I saw it on the television."

The Professor had been reaching for another radish. Now her arm stopped in mid air. "A scorpion!" she exclaimed. She struck her hand against her forehead. "How could I be so stupid? A scorpion . . . Antares!"

"Antares?" Martin repeated.

"It has another name. Alpha Scorpii. It's part of a star system . . . Scorpius, the eighth constellation of the Zodiac. Don't you see? That was the scorpion Tovar was talking about."

"But you can't move a star," Pedro said. "You said it was bigger than the sun. So it's impossible."

"Listen!" The Professor's voice was low. She was almost trembling with excitement. "I thought the lines were a warning, but supposing I was only half right; supposing they were something more than that? You came to Peru looking for a gate, Martin. We still don't know where it is—but if it's closed, there must be something that keeps it closed."

"You mean . . . a sort of lock?" Martin said.

"That's right. Why not a combination lock?"

"I'm lost," Pedro sighed.

"It's simple. The Nazca Lines are a sort of huge time lock. When the stars form the right patterns, only then will the gate open and the Old Ones be free. That's how it works. But the whole purpose of the gate was that it should never open. That's what it was built for."

"And tomorrow night . . ." Martin began.

"Tomorrow night the stars will come close. As close as they'll ever get. Just one star will be missing from the combination. And Tovar means to put something else, something which he calls the golden scorpion in its place."

"But what?" Pedro asked.

Suddenly Martin knew. He remembered the news programme he had heard in England, how the monk had predicted all sorts of twentieth century inventions. He remembered the photographs he had seen in Tovar's office: photographs of outer space, taken from outer space. TC (Lima) stood for Tovar Communications. And what was essential to modern day communications?

"A satellite," he said.

"What?" Pedro asked.

"A satellite," Chambers continued. "An artificial star. Tovar has launched a satellite into outer space and tomorrow night he will position it exactly where Antares ought to be. A golden scorpion instead of the real one. The golden scorpion will complete the pattern of light. The time lock will be activated. And . . ."

"And the gate will open." Martin trembled at the thought.

"That's right. And there's nothing we can do to stop him."

Martin and Pedro looked at the Professor. "Nothing?" Pedro demanded angrily.

"Tovar will be controlling the satellite by radio," Chambers explained. "If we knew the frequency, perhaps we could jam it and move the satellite ourselves. Always assuming we had the necessary equipment, which we don't. The only other way . . ."

"Yes?" Martin said.

"It's hopeless. But if we could get to the transmitter and destroy it, perhaps the satellite would drift off course."

"Why is it hopeless?" Martin asked.

Chambers closed here eyes wearily. "Tovar Communications has its head office in Lima," she said. "But Tovar couldn't operate a satellite from there. There would be too much interference. No. Unless I'm very much mistaken, he'll be in Paracas."

"Where's that?" Martin asked.

"Not too far from here—which also makes it a perfect choice. It's on the coast, about three hundred miles north.

But the trouble is, Martin, Tovar Communications has a major research centre at Paracas. They do a lot of top-secret work there, some of it for the government. The whole place is fenced off—an electrified fence I'll be bound. It's under heavy guard twenty-four hours a day. All the guards are armed. At night there are watch-towers with spotlights. And the grounds are patrolled by savage dogs. It's impossible. You'd need a small army to break into that place."

Martin thought for a moment. Then he got to his feet. When he looked up, there was a grim smile on his face. "A small army?" he said. "I think I may have just the thing." He glanced at Pedro. "We were given a telephone number."

17

The Night of the Scorpion

The car pulled over to the side of the road and Professor
Chambers turned off the ignition. "Well, here we are,"
she said.

"So this is Paracas," Martin muttered.

Paracas was a beautiful bay on the edge of a sparkling
sea. Hundreds of birds—pelicans, flamingoes, gulls and
terns—perched on the shore line or soared over the palm
trees. A smell of flowers hung in the air. Everything was
peaceful. A winding path led down from the road to a
tiny fisherman's port; no more than a cluster of straw-
roofed huts beside a rickety wooden pier. The sun had
set over the sea, streaking the surface with a shimmering
red. Multi-coloured circles rippled around an old ship-
wreck, its hull jutting out of the water, silhouetted
against the horizon.

"That's the port," Chambers said. "The plant is behind us, just over the brow of the hill."

"Right, let's go." Martin opened the door. It was then
that it happened. Pedro had brought Charley with him,
much against the Professor's inclination. He had said
that the monkey got lonely without him and had insisted
that he come along for the ride. Reluctantly, Chambers

had agreed to take care of him while she waited in the car for their return. But, seeing the open door, Charley suddenly sprang forward and before anyone could stop him, he had scurried away over the sand.

"Charley . . . !" Pedro called out. The monkey paused, then ran on. "We've got to find him," he cried.

"We haven't time." Martin looked at his watch. It was nine o'clock. Already the stars were brilliant in the night sky, moving into their deadly position. "Come on, Pedro. He'll be all right."

"I'll look out for the wretched creature," Chambers said.

Together, the two boys moved forward, down into the fisherman's port. The man they had spoken to on the telephone had assured them that their friends would be there at nine o'clock on the dot, but the place seemed deserted. Then Martin pointed. They were there. There were at least forty of them, standing in a line on the edge of the bay, no more than shadows against the sea. The waves lapped at their feet as they waited. Then, as Martin and Pedro approached, one of them stepped forward and raised an arm. It was Tomac.

"You summoned us," he said. "We have come."

"You know what we have to do?" Martin asked.

"We come prepared."

Martin looked at the Incas. They had discarded the ceremonial clothes of Machu Picchu and were now dressed in uniform jeans and black shirts. Yet they carried ancient weapons; bows and arrows, lances, axes and short swords. It was a bizarre mixture of the old and the new, but no warriors could have looked more deadly.

"Then let's go," he said.

"If you see a little monkey," Pedro added, "don't shoot."

They walked back up the path and across the road. Sitting alone in her car, Professor Chambers watched them, hardly able to believe what was happening on the one hand, wishing that it wasn't on the other. With Martin, Pedro and Tomac at the head, the Incas climbed silently up the hill. They paused at the top. Before them, in a small valley, lay the main research centre of Tovar Communications.

It was every bit the fortress that Chambers had described. The compound was square in shape and about the size of a village. Not one but two fences surrounded it, the inner fence carrying brightly painted signs warning that it was electrified. Only one gate led in. It was on the far side of the square, with a wooden hut in front of it and a red-and-white pole across the single concrete road that approached it. Four watch-towers, one at each corner, looked over the compound. The searchlights were already on with their brilliant beams sweeping back and forth across the sand on both sides of the fence.

Martin found himself hypnotized by the beams, following them as, for a brief moment, they lit up sections of the research centre. There were three main buildings at the heart of the compound, surrounded by various smaller structures where the staff must have lived. To one side, there was a circle of tarmac with a helicopter parked in the middle. The searchlight settled on something and Martin's heart leapt. It was a radio installation. Mounted on the roof, a circular bowl revolved slowly, leaning back on its supports, its metal tongue pointing at the stars.

Pedro had seen it too. "Is that it?" he whispered. Martin nodded. "What are all the other buildings?"

"I don't know. Administration, sleeping quarters . . ." The searchlight ran the full length of a low, wooden shed, painted white with a sloping tile roof. "God knows what that is," Martin said.

"How do we get in?" Pedro asked.

"Maybe Tomac has an idea."

"Sssh!" Tomac hissed.

A man had appeared, walking across the sand only a hundred yards away. Tovar was taking no chances. The grounds were being patrolled all round the centre. And the guard had heard them. As they crouched in the sand, Martin and Pedro saw him raise a machine-gun in his hands and creep carefully forward. One shot and it would all be over. Without the advantage of surprise, the Incas would never get near the compound.

Tomac knelt up, holding a sling, a leather pouch on two cords. He took a steel ball from his pocket and began to whirl the sling round until it was moving so fast that it hummed. The guard turned towards the sound. At the same moment, Tomac released the missile. It whistled through the air, striking the man between the eyes. The guard uttered a brief cry and pitched forward. All was silent.

Tomac nodded to himself, then turned round and uttered a command. Two of the Incas sprang forward and began to strip the dead guard of his uniform.

"Now we go round to the gate," he said. "But be careful. No noise."

"Can I have a weapon?" Pedro asked.

"No need. We fight. You wait at gate."

"That's what you think," Martin muttered.

Ten minutes later, the miniature army had reached the other side of the compound and was crouching beside the road in front of the main gate. As Pedro and Martin watched, an Inca, dressed in the guard's uniform, walked up to the gate, limping as if hurt. A voice called out from the shed and the Inca went in. Then there came the sound of a grunt followed by the thump of a body hitting the floor. For a minute everyone froze as a searchlight swept over the shed. Then Tomac motioned with one hand.

Two more men moved forward, carrying bows and arrows. Kneeling back to back beside the road, they aimed upwards in the direction of the two nearest watch-towers. At the same moment, they fired. One of the spotlights careered round, its beam shooting uselessly out to sea. Pedro looked at the other watch-tower. A man appeared, reaching out as if feeling for something in the darkness. Then he toppled forward through the air, an arrow jutting out of his neck.

Now the Incas moved more quickly. It would only be a matter of minutes before the missing guards were discovered. The man in the hut opened the gate and the army entered the compound, immediately making for the cover of the nearest buildings. Even as they ran across the square, however, there was a soft growl and two dogs bounded forward, teeth bared, heckles rising. But the Incas had been prepared for them. Two men raised hollow pipes to their lips and puffed hard. Pedro glimpsed the drugged darts before they hit the dogs. One yelped and lay still. The other staggered forward, then toppled over, hitting the electrified fence. There was a crackle of electricity. Pedro turned his eyes away.

Martin found himself leaning against the wooden wall of the shed he had seen from the hill. Edging forward, he found a small window and peered through. There were people working inside, standing beside benches laden with bottles, tubes and burners. All the scientists— if that's what they were—wore white coats. As he spied on them, one of the men held up a test-tube of white powder and smelt it.

"Cocaine," Tomac whispered. The Inca was right beside him, looking over his shoulder.

"Cocaine . . . ," Martin repeated. "But . . ."

"It's a secret laboratory," Pedro said, peering in through a second window. "Look, Martin!" He pointed at a plastic sack, filled with the same white powder. "It must be worth thousands."

Martin shook his head. "Perhaps it'll help get Richard off the hook," he said. "If the cocaine came from here . . ." He turned to Tomac. "What are you going to do about the radar bowl?" he asked.

"Our business," Tomac replied. "You two stay here."

Perhaps it was the growl of the dogs that had given them away. Perhaps it was the searchlight, still pointing at the sea. Suddenly there was a burst of gun-fire. One of the Incas cried out, jerked backwards and fell. Seconds later, a siren wailed. Doors were flung open and armed men ran out from all directions. Almost before they knew it, Martin and Pedro found themselves in the middle of a pitched battle.

It was impossible to describe what happened next. At first, surprise was still on the side of the Incas. The guards knew that there were intruders in the compound but they didn't know who or where. Had it been otherwise, the battle would have been a short one, the modern weapons of Tavar's men cutting down the Incas with their swords and arrows. But it was dark. The attack was unexpected. Everything was wrapped in confusion.

The small Inca army had split up, sliding into the darkness. About fifty guards had run out of their quarters. Some got no farther than the door. One man appeared directly behind Martin and Pedro, suddenly stepping out of the laboratory. They froze. The guard reached for his pistol. Something whistled through the night air. The guard fell back, the shaft of a spear sticking out of his chest. On the far side of the compound there was a crackle of machine-gun fire and a single scream. Somebody shouted an order. More gun-fire. A figure flitted through the shadows.

"What do we do now?" Pedro asked. The two boys were suddenly alone.

"The radio . . ." Martin said. "That's what we came for."

"But we have no weapons."

"We can start a fire. Or something." Martin knelt in the doorway, leaning over the dead guard. A moment later he stood up. "Here you are," he said. He passed Pedro a gun. "Now let's go . . .!"

The Night of the Scorpion

As Martin ran off, Pedro weighed the gun in his hand, then called after him. "I don't know how to use it!" There was no reply. Shoving the gun into his pocket, Pedro ran after his friend, making for the radar bowl.

He had taken no more than five paces when there was another burst of gun-fire. White flame flashed from one of the two manned observation towers and the sand spat up a few inches in front of him. Pedro dived to one side. Then the world seemed to erupt as a blinding beam of light fixed itself on him. The light paralyzed him. And with a terrific feeling of certainty, he realized that someone in the tower was taking aim at him. Even now, their finger might be squeezing the trigger . . .

A streak of flame soared through the air, then another. Somebody screamed in the watch-tower as the floor and walls caught alight. The light swung away. Blinking, Pedro rolled over and got to his feet, temporarily blinded. Another fire had started in the far corner of the compound and even as his sight returned, he saw two more balls of flame high up in the air. The Incas were shooting fire arrows. But would they be any use against brick and metal?

The same thought was going through Martin's mind as he rested against the wall of the radio station. The radar bowl itself, which had seemed small from a distance, was enormous, towering above him as it revolved on its massive steel supports. The one entrance to the control centre was barred by a thick metal door. It seemed that all their efforts might be for nothing.

A figure stumbled through the darkness. For a moment Martin crouched, searching for cover. Then he recognized Tomac. The Inca had been wounded in the fighting. One blood-streaked arm hung limp by his side. Seeing Martin, he ran forward and paused, panting for breath, by the door.

"How's it going?" Martin asked.

"We lose many people," Tomac replied. "But they

lose more. Now we must hurry. Maybe they telephone for police . . . and army."

"The radar . . ." Martin began.

Tomac nodded and fumbled in a pouch that was strapped across his back. "I bring this," he said.

This was a grenade. It was the sort of thing that Martin had seen in old World War Two films; green with a looped pin at the neck. He wondered where Tomac had got it and was about to ask him when, with a thunderous crash, one of the burning watch-towers toppled and collapsed onto the sand.

"Throw it," he said.

"I can't." The Inca raised his arm. "My arm . . . wounded."

"Then give it to me."

He took the grenade and held it in the palm of his hand. It was lighter than he had imagined. Would it be powerful enough to stop the radar bowl? He looked up. It was still turning slowly. It was a huge target, but it was high up, well above the control centre. What if he missed? At that moment, Pedro arrived. "What's happening?" he demanded.

"Stand back," Martin said.

He lifted the grenade to his mouth and pulled out the pin with his teeth. For a couple of seconds he held it, horribly aware that he was holding a live bomb but at the same time unable to throw it.

"Hurry!" Tomac cried.

Martin twisted round and threw the grenade with all his strength. It hit the side of the radar bowl, rolled round the curving surface and slid into the middle. The three of them crouched low below the wall. Then there was an explosion and a burst of orange flame. Martin looked up. The bowl had stopped turning. The metal tongue was shattered. Their work was over.

"I must go to my men," Tomac said. He hurried away, leaving Martin and Pedro alone again.

Pedro glanced up at the radar bowl. "Good shot, Martin," he said.

"Thanks. I just wish we could get out of here now."

"Me too."

"You're not going anywhere."

The voice had come from the doorway of the radio station. Neither of them had heard the door open. A figure in white trousers and blue blazer stood in the light, looking at them. Martin turned round and began to walk towards him, then stopped as he found himself looking at the muzzle of a heavy, black gun.

"You're not going anywhere," Mr. Todd repeated. His mouth twitched. His snake eyes didn't move. Pedro gazed around him, hoping that one of the Incas might see them. But the fighting had concentrated itself on the other side of the compound. There was no-one in sight. Then he remembered the gun Martin had given him. It was still in his pocket. But he had never used a gun before in his life. The German was a professional killer. He would never have time to draw it out and fire.

"You two children have crossed my path once too often," Mr. Todd continued, "and I have long been looking forward to the day when I could watch you die."

"Killing us won't do any good," Martin gestured at the radar bowl. "You can't control the satellite now."

A smile flickered across Mr. Todd's lips. But still the rest of his face was a cold, expressionless mask. "I have transferred control," he whispered. "Oh, you think you're clever—one of the five. But you see, Mr. Hopkins, the satellite is now being controlled from the Nazca desert, not far from here. In just two hours from now, at midnight exactly, the stars will form their alignment and it will all be over. Of course, you and this Peruvian guttersnipe will be dead and cold by then. Killing you will be a particular pleasure. Even in London you were so cocksure, so arrogant. Well, as you die, remember that it was all for nothing. In just two hours, the gate will open and the Old Ones will return."

Mr. Todd's hands came up, levelling the gun. Almost simultaneously there was a loud screech and something small and brown flashed through the air. The German's shot went wild, ricocheting off a wall. He staggered back, clawing at his face. It was Charley. Somehow the monkey had made its way into the compound. It had been sitting on the roof of the radio station. Now it had leapt onto Mr. Todd's head, its hands pulling at his hair, its arms covering his eyes. Pedro pulled the gun out of his pocket and, clutching it in both hands, pulled the trigger three times. As Charley sprang clear, the bullets tore into the German's chest. Mr. Todd was flung backwards, his own gun spinning away. His body crashed into the wall. For a moment his legs kicked in the sand. Then he lay still.

Pedro dropped the gun. With a whimper, Charley scuffled forward and climbed onto his shoulder. Martin stepped forward and looked at the dead German. In death, expression had at last found a way onto Mr. Todd's face. His eyes were staring and his mouth was open in a picture of sheer astonishment.

Martin turned to Pedro. "Thanks," he said.

"I . . ." Pedro couldn't find the words.

"You had to do it," Martin said. He paused. The gun-shots had stopped. It seemed that the battle was won. "We've got to move," he said. "It isn't over yet."

Tomac pulled at the joystick and Tovar's helicopter lumbered into the air, rocking on a cushion of dust. Martin and Pedro were squeezed into the seat beside him. It was half-past ten. Only ninety minutes were left to them.

They had found the Inca at the gate with what re-mained of his men. Forty-five of them had set out to invade the research centre. Only nineteen remained. But in an uneven contest, they had still won the night. What small number of Tovar's men had survived had fled into the darkness. Hastily, Martin had explained what Mr. Todd had told them. Pedro had been the first to remember the helicopter. Tomac, who had once worked as a pilot, volunteered to take them into the desert for a last, desperate search for Tovar.

Both Martin and Pedro were exhausted. The only thing that kept them going was the thought that after all they had been through, after so many deaths, they couldn't give up. They sat silently as they raced into the desert. The seconds ticked on and the stars moved closer to their pre-ordained pattern.

"How are you feeling, Pedro?" Martin asked.

"I'm OK." Pedro had to shout above the roar of the helicopter. "I told you Charley was dangerous."

"He saved our lives." Martin looked at his watch. "I just hope it was worth it."

"How far is it?" Pedro asked.

"We are over desert now," Tomac said. "Fly over lines."

And then the engine spluttered and stopped.

A stray bullet must have hit the fuel pipe during the fighting. One moment Martin and Pedro were straining to hear what Tomac was saying, the next there was a metallic cough and then a terrifying silence. The helicopter lurched downwards. Pedro found himself pressed tight against the door as the ground rushed up. Tomac scrabbled at the ignition: once, twice, on the third time, the blades began to turn again and the helicopter tilted in the air. But it was too late. The back wheel hit the sand. There was an explosive crack as the blades snapped and the front window shattered into a mass of of glittering pieces. They were thrown forward as the sand rushed at them in a wave. Then everything blacked out.

Pedro was the first to recover. He woke up to find himself lying on the sand a few yards away from the wreckage of the helicopter. Miraculously, he was unhurt. The helicopter was burning now, the flames spreading fast. Getting to his feet, he stumbled towards the cockpit, fighting for breath as the smoke billowed around him. The heat was terrific. Any second now the reserve fuel tank would explode, but he had to look inside first to find Martin and Tomac . . .

The Inca was dead, slumped over the controls, blood pouring from terrible wounds in his neck. For a moment Pedro feared that Martin too had been killed. He was lying across the seat, hanging half out of the helicopter, his body covered in fragments of glass. But he was still breathing. Pedro grabbed hold of his friend and pulled him out of the cockpit. The flames seemed to leap out as if trying to grab hold of him.But he was away, pulling Martin along the sand. He took about ten paces. Then the helicopter exploded. Pedro was thrown down with burning sand whipping into his back.

Martin lay with his eyes closed, his breath hard and uneven. His clothes were torn, his arms and legs streaked with burn marks. The force of the impact, which had thrown Pedro clear, had dashed him against the controls and his shoulder was bruised and swollen. But to Pedro's relief, his eyes suddenly flickered open.

"Martin," he said urgently, "I'm going to get help. OK? Maybe a car will come. Do you understand?

Martin tried to speak. An unpleasant rattle came from his lips.

"Don't talk," Pedro said. "And don't move. Just lie still. I'll be back soon."

Pedro ran. He was unconscious of anything but the soft shuffling of his feet in the sand and the rasp of his breath in his ears. Above him, the stars shone brightly, casting a silver light over the desert. He had seen the main highway from the helicopter only seconds before the crash. Now he made for it, praying that his instincts were taking him in the right direction.

He ran until his legs hurt him. Sweat trickled down underneath his shirt and he could feel blisters on his feet. Then, when he thought he could go no farther, he saw the road and, better still, a car parked on the sand beside it. As he drew closer, he saw that it wasn't a car but a lorry; a lorry with something strapped to its roof.

"Hello!" he shouted, pressing forward.

He felt hard concrete underneath his feet as he reached the road. Now he could hear the whine of machinery and the hum of a generator, both of them coming from the lorry. There was a light shining out of its open back. Even as he reached the lorry, he realized what it was, what he had stumbled upon. But it was too late to go back.

Four guns were pointed at him.

"Hello, young man," Victor Valenzuela de Tovar said. "How very nice of you to join us."

18
The Gate Opens

Martin stood up. He felt sick. His head was burning, but still he shivered in the cool night air. He could feel the sweat glistening on his forehead. "Pedro . . . ?" he muttered. He was answered by silence. Vaguely he remembered what had happened. The helicopter had crashed. Pedro had gone to get help. He was alone in the middle of the desert.

He stepped forward and cried out with pain. His right shoulder had been completely numb—until he moved it. Behind him, the last flames were dying out on the wreckage of the helicopter. He wanted to rest, to stay where he was, but something urged him forward. Each movement brought a new stab of pain, but still he went on.

He had no idea where he was going, but the irresistible power that led him seemed to steer him in one direction. He had become no more than a puppet. Other forces controlled him. Faster and faster his legs carried him until he was running, his mind blank, his eyes unseeing. At last he slowed down. Almost crying with relief, he staggered to a halt, swayed and stood still. Then he realized where he was.

He had returned to the platform. He knew it before

he recognized the flat, square shape, stark in the moonlight. The sign that he knew and dreaded seemed to burn black. Unwillingly, he stepped onto it.

Above him, the stars were bright, the light unnatural. Far away on the horizon, he could make out the gap between the two mountain ranges that bordered the desert. He remembered what the Professor had told him. That was where the missing star should be. But all was dark. It was as if there were a great hole in space. The deadly pattern of stars was incomplete.

A movement caught his eye. He looked round. A star was moving in the sky. At least, it looked like a star. It was larger and brighter than the others, and it seemed to be moving at a fantastic speed. As it moved, it grew even brighter until it had taken on the appearance of a blazing comet. Martin felt the touch of fear.

The golden scorpion was being guided towards the gap in the mountains, and nothing could stop it.

"I don't think I actually know your name," Victor Valenzuela de Tovar said.

"I'm Pedro."

"Ah, Pedro! What a charming name. And what a fortunate moment to arrive. Ten to twelve. You just have time to look around. I'm sure you'll be impressed."

The inside of the lorry had been fitted out like a miniature laboratory, fed by a generator set up in the sand about a hundred yards away. Row upon row of complicated machinery had been stacked up, one box on top of the other. Dozens of buttons and dials, a maze of plugs and wires, lines of flashing lights and flowing indicator panels covered the gleaming metal faces. The object on top of the lorry, he now realized, had been the bowl of a second, smaller radar.

Tovar swung round in his chair and smiled at him. Sitting there, with his feet dangling over the floor, the industrialist looked like nothing more than an insane child with an incredible toy.

"Was that your helicopter just now?" he asked.

Pedro nodded. "Yes."

"I saw it go down. Quite a bang! And your friend, the Hopkins boy, he was killed in the crash?"

"No. He needs help. He'll die if I don't get back to him."

The industrialist sighed. "He'll die anyway. Forget him. We still have a little time together. I don't know who you are or how you got mixed up in this, but I'm glad you've come, really I am. Let me tell you how clever I've been."

Pedro looked around him. Two of the Indians who had chased him in Cuzco stood in the lorry, covering him with their guns. Two more had been guarding the generator. Now they were behind him, watching him carefully. The generator . . . it was his only chance. But there was no way he could move. He would have to wait for an opportunity.

"All right," he said. "You tell me what you want to. But then you must let me get back to Martin."

The industrialist shrugged. "Very well." There was mockery in his voice.

"As you have probably guessed," Tovar began, "the Nazca Lines are a sort of magic time-lock. I have found a way to break the combination." He giggled proudly. "It was I who first realized the truth. For years I searched for the platform, the focusing point that would give me the key I needed. Then the diary of the mad monk turned up. I would have paid a million pounds for that diary. But in the end I got it for nothing.

"Once I had read the diary, I realized that although the stars would come close to the right combination, they wouldn't come quite close enough. But the monk gave me the answer. He had predicted the coming of satellites just as Nostradamus—I doubt if you've heard of Nostradamus, you don't seem very well educated to me—just as he had predicted the atom bomb, the aeroplane . . . and so on.

"Now it just so happened that as head of Tovar Communications I had not just one satellite in my control but several. Even if I hadn't, I could have bought one. I'm terribly rich, you know." He clapped his hands together excitedly. "The Golden Scorpion was actually built for the USA government, under contract. It was built to take photographs of Russia and places like that. But I had other plans for it.

"Do you know much about satellites, Pedro? I don't suppose you do, so let me tell you. Every single day the Russians and the Americans spend twenty-five million pounds on them. Even as we speak, there are hundreds of satellites orbiting the earth, and they're all up there for the same reason. War. I'm told that a new satellite leaves the earth every four days.

"It's a deadly game, Pedro. There are spy satellites; anti-ballistic missile satellites; high energy lasers; electro-magnetic pulses. The night sky may look beautiful to you on a summer evening. But it's a battlefield where a single button can release a thousand deaths. So don't you think it's right and proper that a satellite will be the key to unlock the Old Ones? They really are the weapons of death.

"I launched the Golden Scorpion a week ago. I am controlling it from this mobile laboratory. Mr. Todd brought it in from the Pacific using the stronger radio signal at the research centre. But now it's close enough to be in range. I fired the retroactive rockets to move it to an exact position above the Nazca Lines just a few minutes before you dropped in. And now it is two minutes to twelve. Soon the Old Ones will be back. Soon a new, better world will begin. So tell me, Pedro; aren't I clever? What do you think?"

Pedro had listened to this with growing fear. Now he spoke. "I think you're a little bit mad," he said.

The industrialist almost screamed with rage. "Don't call me that! Never call me that!" He quietened down. "I don't like being called little!"

"Let me go and get help for Martin," Pedro said.

Tovar looked at him sadly. "You know I can't let you leave here," he said.

"But you promised."

"I know. It was naughty of me. But the boy has to die. So do you." He laughed. "You must see that. You're both enemies of the Old Ones."

Victor Valenzuela de Tovar reached out and turned a dial. With another hand he flicked a row of switches. "But enough of this chat," he said. "It is one minute to twelve. The time has come."

The artificial star moved steadily nearer. Martin had forgotten his pain. He could sense an extraordinary change in the desert. It had become terribly cold, with icy gusts of wind stabbing across the sand. The light from the stars had intensified until it was a hard glare. The feeling of menace was so distinct that he could almost touch it. It was all around him. And, just as the Inca had predicted, he was facing it alone.

The menace. Suddenly Martin knew. At last he understood where the great gate of the Nazca desert was located. He had thought it would be a circle of stones, a small, recognizable structure. But the gate *was* the desert. The Nazca Lines and the Nazca gate were one and the same thing. He had read about it, flown over it and walked on it but until now he had never seen it. And now it was too late.

The satellite passed over the last mountain peak, slowed down and came to a rest between the two ranges. The pattern was complete, the combination broken.

Nothing happened. For a moment, Martin wondered if after all the gate was going to remain closed, unaffected by the stars. Then a soft rumbling reached his ears. It came from beyond the horizon, beneath the horizon, from all around him. It could have been the sound of a plane flying close overhead, but underneath the cobweb of stars the sky was clear.

A horrible smell filled the desert air. It was the smell of rotting meat, sweet and sickly. Martin looked across the sand. Some sort of liquid, as thick as tar but dark green, was spreading over the desert. It seemed to stretch out like tentacles in every direction, gleaming in the silver light. Even as he watched, circles and triangles formed, followed by giant, incomprehensible signs. Then he knew that the tar was oozing out of the lines themselves, that the Nazca Lines were breaking up.

The rumbling grew louder, the cold wind stronger. Martin was almost deafened, his hair flapping against his forehead. He lost his balance and staggered. The platform had moved. As he twisted round, the whole desert began to shake. His vision shimmered and the mountains trembled as a roaring wind buffeted into him like an invisible fist, a whirlwind of sand lashing his hands and face.

Then there was a loud crack and light burst out of the desert floor, rising up out of the lines and slicing through the night. Far beneath him there was a howl, a cry of triumph, as the first of the Old Ones prepared to pass through the opening gate.

Pedro felt the earthquake, heard the rumbling. His face was filled with anger and helplessness. The four Indians were still covering him, two outside the mobile laboratory, two inside. If he took a single step forward, they would shoot him down.

Victor Valenzuela de Tovar laughed with excitement, his eyes dancing. "It's begun!" he cried. "Soon my masters will have returned. Soon! Soon!"

Desperately Pedro looked around him: at the door of the lorry hanging open, at the two Indians on the sand, and at the fire extinguisher strapped to the wall a few feet in front of him. Swallowing hard, he realized that he had to act. He had nothing to lose.

A sudden shock-wave hit the lorry, almost toppling it. The two Indians standing inside were thrown off balance, one knocking into the other. The doors of the lorry swung shut. At that moment, Pedro sprang forward. His hands reached the handles of the doors and turned them. With a feeling of relief, he felt the lock connect, cutting off the two Indians outside. That left only three to one.

He seized the fire extinguisher, tore it away from the wall and pounded it against the floor. As the Indians tried to straighten up inside the shaking lorry, he pointed the nozzle at them, blinding them with a jet of white foam. The lorry swayed as a second shock-wave hit it. Getting a firm grip with his feet, Pedro swung the fire extinguisher, the heavy cylinder crashing into the side of the nearer Indian's head. The man crumpled without a sound. He turned to face the second Indian, just in time to see the gun pointing at him. Instinctively, he raised the fire extinguisher. There was an explosion and, simultaneously, a clang as the bullet bounced off the cylinder. Then Pedro charged forward, using the fire extinguisher as a battering ram. He caught the Indian in the chest, sending him hurtling into the machines. The man's elbow broke through a panel with a tinkle of glass. There was a blue flash. The Indian screamed. For a moment his eyes went white. Then the life went out of him and he collapsed on the floor.

Dropping the fire extinguisher, Pedro threw himself forward, reaching out for the Indian's gun. His fingers touched the barrel but then there was a blast of pain behind his eyes as the industrialist's foot cracked into his head. The strength drained out of his body. He rolled over and dragged himself to his knees, trying to shake the brilliant pin-pricks of light away from him. When his vision cleared, he saw Victor Valenzuela de Tovar holding the gun a few inches away. There was nothing more he could do.

A jagged streak of bright red light had torn through the sky. It was as if the skin of the night had been ripped away to reveal the flesh and blood beneath. Far below, the lines had widened, knife blades of light cutting across the desert. Martin was almost blind, a torrent of sand spiralling around him. The rumbling had grown into a fantastic booming, the sound hammering in his ears.

There was an eruption of crimson light in the mountains. The tallest peak had shattered, a thousand splinters of rock whirling into the night followed by a dense cloud of grey smoke. The whole mountain shuddered. Then a glowing trickle of lava appeared at the rim, slowly snaking downwards to the desert. A second mountain blew apart. Fireballs cascaded through the air. Soon the entire pampas was surrounded by a wall of smoke that seemed to reach up as far as the stars themselves.

The subterranean howling continued. The liquid frothed and bubbled. Now huge gaps were appearing in the desert floor as slowly, majestically, the great triangles opened inwards. White light flooded out as the surface of the desert sank. The howling grew even louder. Then the first of the Old Ones appeared.

It was in the shape of a bird but it was the size of a house. With slowly beating wings, it soared into the air, two massive sets of claws hanging under it. Farther away, a gigantic spider pulled itself over the edge of the abyss, its eyes glowing a deadly green. With a chilling laugh, a gigantic monkey bounced onto the sand, its tail twisting and curling, its teeth arched in a grotesque smile.

Some of the Old Ones were like no recognizable life form: weird shapes with the beginnings of limbs stretching out of them. Soon the whole desert floor was swarming with them, but still they came, an army of death and destruction. They came in many sizes, but all of them were black, shrouded by a silvery mist that separated them from the real world. For a moment they paused on the desert floor, breathing the Earth air for the first time in a million years. Then they bounded forward, disappearing into the swirling clouds of smoke and sand.

A fork of lightning splintered through the sky and the rumbling deepened. Figures in the form of men were appearing, some carrying spears and axes, others on horseback, clad in armour. They too were black— shadowmen. Some dank and rotten material covered their bodies. Yet behind their ragged coverings, Martin could see the glow of their eyes and even in the tempest he could make out the white smoke of their breath curling around their lips. He had never seen them before, not even in his nightmares, but he knew what they were. The advance guard for the King of the Old Ones.

Martin took a deep breath and closed his eyes. The time, he knew, was very near. Now he searched for the power within him, the power that had destroyed the condors only two nights before.Once again he felt it stirring, a tingling in the pit of his stomach that seemed to ripple through his blood. The wind howled about his head and the sand beat at him as he drew on the power, feeding it, willing it on. He could feel it building up, flowing into his arms.

He opened his eyes and looked up.

Orange flames burst out of the machinery, wires sparked and glass panels shattered. Victor Valenzuela de Tovar took aim with his gun but, at the same moment, the mobile laboratory was rocked once again, this time teetering so far to one side that Pedro was sure it would topple over. The industrialist tumbled backwards before he could pull the trigger, dropping the gun. Behind him, a television monitor slid off the bench and smashed onto the floor, flickering wires trailing behind it. Overhead there was a grinding tear as the wind caught the radar and pulled it off the roof.

With a cry of rage, the industrialist turned his back on Pedro and groped for the doors. As the flames ran wild, filling the interior with acrid smoke, he flung them open and dropped onto the sand outside. Pedro got to his feet, his eyes watering, choking for breath. Staggering forward, he found the doors and followed the industrialist out into the desert.

Outside, the world had gone mad. The sand had turned into a furious sea. Jagged ribbons of unnatural red and green zig-zagged through the sky. The wind roared. Huge trenches had appeared in the ground as the desert broke up in the grip of the earthquake. Pedro looked around for the other two Indians but it was impossible to see more than a few feet away. Behind him, the lorry exploded in flames, the metal buckling, the machinery disintegrating. He took a few steps back, the ground vibrating beneath his feet, one hand up to protect his eyes from the tornado of sand.

Suddenly there was a cry behind him and before he could react a silver rod was looped over his head, driving into his throat. He tried to catch his breath, but the grip was too tight. Tovar was behind him, both hands clutching a length of metal from the top of the lorry. He pulled tighter, strangling Pedro.

Pedro reached back, trying to get hold of the industrialist. His fingers clawed at the metal that was pressing into his throat. He fought for breath. But it was hopeless. Already the strength had gone out of him. The blood throbbed behind his eyes and darkness rushed in. He fell to his knees.

But even as he slipped towards the ground, it

disappeared. It was as if he were watching his own grave
being dug. The earthquake had strengthened its hold on
the desert. Another long trench had torn through the
ground, the sand cascading inwards. And Pedro and
Tovar had been right in its path. Now the two of them
plunged into the void. As they fell, the industrialist
screamed and at the same moment the grip around
Pedro's throat loosened and the metal rod fell away.
Then they hit the bottom.

The trench was about ten feet deep, a narrow corridor
that ran on for miles in each direction beneath the desert.
Sand poured down in torrents from above and even as
Pedro stood up, the two walls shivered and moved
inwards. With a rush of fear, he realized that the trench
was about to close up as quickly as it had opened. If he
couldn't find a way out, he would be buried alive.

There was a groan behind him. Victor Valenzuela de
Tovar lay on his side, one leg sticking out at a horrible
angle. But Pedro had no time to spare. The walls shook
again and moved in a little more. They were too soft to
climb, but then he saw his one way out; the cable that
had connected the generator to the lorry hung down
from the surface.

The sides of the trench shuddered again. Pedro ran
forward and seized hold of the cable. The passage was
now so narrow that he could have touched both walls
with his outstretched hands. He pulled himself upwards.
His heart lurched as the cable dropped back six inches
and for a moment he dangled in space. But the cable
held.

Using the last reserves of his strength, he climbed
again, gasping with relief as he pulled himself over the
edge of the chasm.

"Pedro!"

He looked down. Somehow the industrialist had got
to his feet. He was holding onto the cable, his face grey,
his eyes wide with fear.

"Pedro!" he called again. "I've broken my leg. I can't pull myself up."

The walls closed a few more inches. Tears streamed down Tovar's face. "Please help me!" he pleaded. "Don't leave me in this horrible place!"

Pedro wanted to ignore him, to turn his back on him and forget him. But he knew he couldn't. Reluctantly, he lay on his stomach, holding the cable for support, his body jutting out over the trench.

"Get my hand," he called down. "I'll pull you up."

The walls shook once more and the corridor narrowed farther. Victor Valenzuela de Tovar reached out. But his fingers were six inches away from Pedro's hand. "I can't reach!" he cried. "I can't . . ."

"Try!" Pedro shouted.

The industrialist strained with every muscle. "No!" he screamed. "I can't! I'm too . . ."

At last the walls closed. Pedro rolled away as Victor Valenzuela de Tovar let out one last cry, abruptly cut off as the sand pounded down on him, drowning him. The two sides of the trench met.

Pedro stood up. His throat was bruised and swollen, his head throbbing where he had been kicked. But the desert was silent. The wind had fallen. The earthquake had subsided. Above, the sky was clear, the streaks of colour fading. A few yards away, the crumpled lorry lay on its side, smoke trickling out of the twisted metal. There was no-one else in sight.

Slowly, he began to walk back along the road.

Martin was still standing on the platform, but he was no longer alone. The armies of the Old Ones surrounded him, forming two vast circles. The animals made up the outer ring, feathers and hair fluttering in the breeze. A closer, inner ring contained the horsemen; black, ghost-like figures on skeletal mounts. Spear carriers stood between them, their black hands clutching ugly lengths of iron. The smell of death was all about them. Though some of the creatures had human form, there was nothing remotely human about them. They had come from another time, another world. They were dead. And death was their only pleasure.

Then the King of the Old Ones rose silently out of the desert floor.

Martin trembled. The King was huge, bigger than anything he had ever seen. Even his curving finger-nails were larger than Martin. In colour he was black, though tinged with a dark, sea-weed green. His eyes burned red. Darkness clung to the terrible creature like a cloak, obscuring him. Martin was aware of a spiked band around his wrist and a horned helmet and crown on his head. He could just make out glistening scales along his arms. He could see the thick tail, resting in the sand. But all these were merely glimpsed in the darkness. The King of the Old Ones was too gigantic, too awesome to be seen.

"Go back!" Martin shouted. His voice was tiny, the cry of an insect. "You have no place here!"

The King of the Old Ones laughed, a dreadful, dry laugh that began deep inside him and echoed all around.

"Go back!" Martin cried again. He raised his arms. The power surged through him. He hurled it towards the creature.

The white beams burst out of the palms of his hands, shooting towards it. They hit the King of the Old Ones in the side of the neck. He stepped back, his eyes flaming, his webbed hands clawing at the air. Martin, a mere speck in front of him, pushed harder, concentrating his power. Then the King of the Old Ones screamed, a scream that was taken up by all his creatures as they suffered his pain and shared his defeat.

Three miles away, Pedro heard the scream and turned. Shutting his eyes, he braced himself on the road, willing himself next to Martin, channelling his own power across the desert that separated them. Now he could sense it inside him, growing, thrusting out. Raising his arms, he stretched out his hands.

"Martin!" he cried.

Martin heard him and felt his power surge forward, stronger than ever. Now the assembled army was crying out with fear as well as pain as their master writhed before them. Slowly, bellowing with rage, the King of the Old Ones sank back into the ground, unable to endure the force of Martin's power. And as he went, the creatures seemed to wither up, shrivelling like scraps of paper in a bonfire. Suddenly it was over as quickly as it had begun. The beams faltered and died away. The desert was empty.

Martin stood alone once more, swaying on his feet. He had taken his power to the limit and it had burnt him up. He saw two suns, seering his eyes. Then the night thundered towards him and darkness overwhelmed him.

He fell onto the platform and lay still.

19

The Healer

"I'm sorry, Mr. Cole," Professor Chambers said. "Martin is dying. There's nothing more we can do for him."

Richard Cole sat in silence as the Professor drove him from Nazca airstrip. During the journey, she ran quickly through what had happened to Martin since the journalist had been arrested. It was three days since the Incas had found him lying in the desert, surrounded by the ruins of the lines. The Nazca Lines had been totally obliterated by the earthquake. The desert was pitted with craters. Hills had blistered up where once the sand had been flat. One of the great mysteries of the ancient world had vanished for ever.

Richard had finally been released from prison that morning. The influence of the Professor's friends, the discovery of the cocaine factory in Tovar's research centre and the earthquake itself with all its implications had been enough to make the Peruvian authorities glad to be rid of him. Chambers had sent him a telegram at the prison. He had taken the first available flight to Nazca.

"Martin was taken to the local hospital," Professor Chambers continued as they turned into the drive of her house. "He's been in a coma from the time he was found. After they'd patched up his wounds—he damaged his shoulder in the helicopter crash and he was a mass of cuts and bruises—I had him brought home. I hired a trained nurse to sit with him. I hoped having him near might help." She shook her head. "But he just gets weaker by the hour. I still don't know what happened to him out in the desert, Mr. Cole, but it's as if . . . as if his life has been drained out of him."

The car stopped and Richard got out. "Can I see him?" he asked.

"Of course. But be prepared for the worst."

"Sure."

"I'm really sorry, Mr. Cole."

"You've done everything you could, Professor." Richard sighed. "I'm really grateful. But now I just want to see him."

Martin had been put to bed on the second floor. The nurse was sitting just outside the open door. It was a quiet room with rush mats on the floor and bright plaster walls. The windows were all open but shutters had been drawn across them to keep the place cool. A fan turned on a small table. Martin lay in bed, covered by a single sheet. Softly, Richard walked up to him. As he looked down on his friend, he felt a tightness in his throat. Martin was very close to death. A plastic bag hung above the bed, a transparent fluid dripping down through a tube that had been injected into his emaciated arm. His face was pale, his eyes closed. The rise and fall of his chest as he breathed was so slight as to be almost imperceptible.

"Has he eaten anything?" Richard asked.

"No." Professor Chambers moved forward. "He's been on a drip for three days."

Richard turned away. "What about his friend?" he asked. "The other boy . . . Pedro."

"Pedro's still at the hospital. We found him on the

road about an hour before we picked up Martin. He's been treated for second degree burns, concussion and God knows what else. He's been half-strangled, kicked ..." The Professor sniffed. "I visited him yesterday afternoon but he was asleep. It'll be at least another week before he's allowed out."

The words were no sooner out of her mouth than the nurse in the corridor cried out and the door swung open. Professor Chambers stared. Pedro was there, still in his pyjamas, his head wrapped in bandages, propping himself up against the wall for support.

"What on earth do you think ... ?" she began.

Pedro held up a hand. "You must leave now," he said. "Martin needs me."

"What do you mean?"

"There's no time to explain."

"But you're ill, child!"

"I'm OK now. I have to help Martin. Please, Professor! Do what I say."

Pedro staggered over to the bed and sat down on its edge. For a moment he looked at Martin. Then, closing his eyes, he reached out with one hand, his fingers spread in the shape of a star. Gently, he laid the hand on Martin's forehead, his own brown skin in sharp contrast with Martin's pallor. Chambers pursed her lips. Then she took Richard's arm and led him outside, closing the door gently behind her.

"Thaumaturgy," she said as she sat down with him on the verandah.

"What?" Richard asked.

"Faith healing." She poured two glasses of iced fruit juice from a jug. "I've come across it in books, but this is the first time I've seen it. Thaumaturgy is the ability to treat sickness using some sort of inner, psychic power. It played an important part in the Inca civilization."

"But Pedro ..."

"Young Pedro just happens to be some sort of Inca chieftain himself, Richard."

"How do you know that?"

"The Incas told me. I don't pretend to understand it all, but I managed to speak to them before they all disappeared again." She picked up her glass. "Don't underestimate Pedro, Richard. If anyone can help Martin, he can."

Nonetheless, they spent two anxious hours on the verandah before the nurse ran out excitedly, summoning them upstairs. Hurriedly they went, Richard taking the staircase three steps at a time. Only at Martin's door did he pause and prepare himself. Then he opened the door.

Martin was sitting up in bed with his eyes open. As he saw Richard, he smiled. Feeling the relief course through him, Richard ran forward. Professor Chambers went over to Pedro who was standing beside the window. He looked exhausted, but he too was smiling. Richard reached out and grasped his friend's hand.

"Martin," he muttered.

"Hello, Richard," Martin said. His voice was weak and his face was gaunt and pale but the life was back in his eyes.

Martin beckoned to Pedro who came over and sat on the other side of the bed. He turned to Richard. "You haven't met Pedro," he said, speaking slowly and quietly. "He has power like mine. He healed my leg in Lima. He even heals monkeys. And now he's come and done it again." His head fell back against the pillow and he prepared to sleep. "Richard . . ." he muttered. "Meet Pedro. He's one of the five."

As the sun dipped down behind the houses, a soft golden light settled on the town of Nazca. A quarter moon hung pale in the sky with just one solitary star for company.

A dog barked in the street. Then suddenly everything was quiet.

Martin lay in a hammock in the garden of the Professor's house. Two goats wandered slowly across the lawn. Everything was so tranquil that it was hard to believe that the terrible night in the desert had really happened. But two weeks had passed since then. Two weeks of rest and recovery.

Pedro was sitting in a chair near him. Since Martin had come out of the coma, he had seldom left his side. They heard a door open and Professor Chambers stepped out onto the verandah. Seeing the two boys, she waved and crossed the lawn.

"How are you feeling this evening?" she asked.

"I'm fine," Martin said. "I feel stronger every day."

"You shouldn't stay out too long," Professor Chambers said. "It's beginning to get cool."

"Where's Richard?" Pedro asked.

"Inside, sorting out his things. Now that the three of you have decided to stay here for a while, I've given you all rooms in the guest-house. You'll be more comfortable there and you'll be out of my way when I'm working. At the moment, your possessions are spread out over three beds, two carpets and the lawn. I'm afraid Richard isn't exactly organised."

Professor Chambers had brought a shooting-stick with her. She opened it and sat down.

"All I can say," she muttered, "is that I'm really looking forward to a bit of peace and quiet."

"I only hope you're right," Martin said.

She looked at him sternly. "What do you mean?"

Martin glanced at Pedro, then he turned to face the Professor. "I've told you what happened, that night in the desert," he began. "But I've been thinking about it a lot since then. I can't stop thinking about it."

"Well that's perfectly understandable," the Professor said.

"I wouldn't have been strong enough to defeat the Old Ones by myself," Martin continued. "Not once they'd broken through the gate. But Pedro helped me. Together, we had the power to drive them back."

His eyes wandered across the garden, searching through the shadows. When he spoke again, his voice was barely more than a whisper. "But did we have the power to close the gate?" he asked. "Did we stop the Old Ones for good? Or have we only gained time? *Perhaps the gate is still open. Perhaps they'll come back . . .*"

It was dark now, but as they watched, the stars returned, one after another until the whole sky was ablaze with pinpricks of light. Something dropped out of a tree and landed on the Professor's head. Chambers screamed and almost fell off her shooting-stick. It was Charley. Pedro's monkey had taken to its new home with gusto and although the Professor was constantly swearing she would have it shot, the monkey seemed to have developed an extraordinary fondness for her.

Despite themselves, Pedro and Martin couldn't help laughing. The Professor stood up with Charley still squatting on her head. "It's dinner soon," she said. "Let's go in . . ."

"I'm starving," Martin said.

"Me too," Pedro agreed.

Suddenly, from the side of the house, there was a great cry. It was Richard. He shouted again. Then, as the servants scurried round to see what had happened, they heard him exclaim in fluent Spanish:

"Una cabra se comió mi passaporte!"

"What now?" Chambers asked, picking up the shooting-stick.

Martin laughed again. "It's only Richard," he said. "I think a goat has just eaten his passport."